THE SECRET LANGUAGE OF BIRDS

THE SECRET LANGUAGE OF BIRDS

LYNNE KELLY

DELACORTE PRESS

Text copyright © 2024 by Lynne Kelly
Jacket art copyright © 2024 by Leo Nickolls

All rights reserved. Published in the United States by Delacorte Press, an imprint of Random House Children's Books, a division of Penguin Random House LLC, New York.

Delacorte Press is a registered trademark and the colophon is a trademark of Penguin Random House LLC.

Visit us on the Web! rhcbooks.com

Educators and librarians, for a variety of teaching tools, visit us at RHTeachersLibrarians.com

Library of Congress Cataloging-in-Publication Data is available upon request.
ISBN 978-1-5247-7027-3 (hardcover) — ISBN 978-1-5247-7028-0 (lib. bdg.) —
ISBN 978-1-5247-7029-7 (ebook)

The text of this book is set in 12.5 -point Macklin.
Interior design by Ken Crossland

Printed in the United States of America
10 9 8 7 6 5 4 3 2 1
First Edition

For those who protect the cranes

This book is also dedicated to the Uvalde, Texas, families of:

Nevaeh Alyssa Bravo

Jacklyn "Jackie" Jaylen Cazares

Makenna Lee Elrod

Jose Manuel Flores Jr.

Eliahna "Ellie" Amaya Garcia

Irma Garcia

Uziyah "Uzi" Sergio Garcia

Amerie Jo Garza

Xavier James Lopez

Jayce Carmelo Luevanos

Tess Marie Mata

Maranda Gail Mathis

Eva Mireles

Alithia Haven Ramirez

Annabell Guadalupe Rodriguez

Maite Yuleana Rodriguez

Alexandria "Lexi" Aniyah Rubio

Layla Salazar

Jailah Nicole Silguero

Eliahna Torres

Rojelio Fernando Torres

They deserved more time for adventures.

Chapter 1

If not for the bird, I'd have been in the car with my family instead of standing in a gas station parking lot. Not that I'm blaming the bird for what happened. It wasn't his fault.

I stared down Highway 290, wondering how far my family would drive before noticing they were one kid short of a full minivan.

This wasn't a regular gas station with a little convenience store and a rack of chips. Nothing that pathetic. Buc-ee's needs an entire wall just for all their flavors of beef jerky. It's a huge place with aisle after aisle of snacks, a fudge counter, a café, toys, T-shirts, and even stuff for decorating the house. My mom thought the sequined cattle skulls with flowers in the eye sockets were tacky, but we did have one of the big metal stars on our living room wall. And Buc-ee's was the only place Mom would stop for a restroom break on a road trip. They're famous for their restrooms. The Buc-ee's beaver mascot shows up on billboards along the freeway, announcing things like RISK IT FOR THE BRISKET! and 75 MILES TO BUC-EE'S! YOU CAN HOLD IT! And even if I thought, "No, I absolutely cannot hold it," I'd have to wait anyway, because we were not stopping anywhere else.

My point is, if you're going to be abandoned someplace, you could do a lot worse than Buc-ee's.

We were on our way home to Houston after a long weekend at a lake house in Austin. As soon as we parked at a gas pump, Mom and Dad each grabbed one of the twins, since they were overdue for diaper changes. Chloe and Aiden were almost potty-trained, but that "almost" is important when you're trying to make it between Buc-ee's stops.

"You kids stick together," Mom said to the rest of us— that meant me and my sixteen-year-old sister, Sage, and my brother, Declan, who was fourteen, just a year older than me. Mom handed a credit card to Sage and said, "Go ahead and order the sandwiches. We'll meet you back here at the car."

Declan and I got our fountain drinks, pressing our cups under each spout to get a mixture of all the flavors. Sage usually did the same. But this time, she set her cup down and wandered over to the refrigerated cases, where some guys who looked like football players were picking out sports drinks. I followed her while sipping my drink. It tasted pretty good, even though I'd overdone it on the Fanta orange.

"Could you reach a Dr Pepper for me?" Sage asked one of the boys. She pointed to the top shelf.

"Why aren't you getting your own drink?" I asked.

She glared at me and said, "I just want a can of Dr Pepper, okay?" Her eyes were wide, like she was trying to send me a secret message. "And I need someone to reach it for me."

"Pretty sure I could reach that."

She turned back to the guys and said, "My little sister," while shaking her head. Then she tossed her hair and gave a huge smile to the guy who'd handed her the drink. "Thank you *so* much," she said, really cheerful, like he'd given her a winning lottery ticket.

"You're being weird," I told her as Declan came up next to me.

Sage laughed, then handed me the credit card. "Here, why don't y'all go order the sandwiches?"

"Mom said we have to stay together."

"I'll catch up to you," she said. "You can handle this, right? Just order what everyone likes."

Declan and I found an available touch screen at the café and put in the sandwich orders. BBQ brisket for him, chicken croissant for me, a grilled cheese cut into quarters for Chloe and Aiden to share, pastrami Reuben for Dad, and a turkey club for Mom. I punched in a ham and cheese for Sage, with extra pickles. Sage hated pickles.

"I'm going to look at the snacks," said Declan.

"Mom and Dad aren't going to buy you any Beaver Nuggets."

"Geez, Nina, I'm just going to look. Can you wait for the sandwiches?"

"Fine."

Sage and the football pack had moved on to the jerky wall. She giggled and gave one of them a playful slap to the shoulder. "Perfect," I mumbled. "Bunch of jerks at the jerky wall." My face flushed with embarrassment, even though no one could hear me. I was acting like a little kid. Maybe I'd act like Sage when I was older. After another glance in her direction, I shook my head, unable to picture it. Why laugh at something that's not even funny? Not that I could overhear what the guys were saying, but it probably wasn't that funny.

After a few minutes, "Order for Nina" came through the overhead speaker. A woman wearing a white apron over her Buc-ee's T-shirt and khakis was working at the ice cream counter next to the sandwich pickup. Her gray curls were squished beneath a hairnet. While scooping ice cream with one hand, she leaned over and slid the bag of sandwiches closer to me.

"You got it, sweetie?" she said. "That's a big order." A plastic name tag on her shirt read WANDA.

"Thanks. I've got it."

Dad came up to the counter then, holding Chloe by the hand. She'd undone her pigtails, as usual, leaving her hair sticking up like a pile of white cotton candy on her head. "There you are," said Dad. "Where are Declan and Sage?"

I handed him the card and the bag and pointed to Sage. "And Declan's looking at snacks."

"Go tell him the Barlow bus is headin' out."

On the way to fetch Declan, I noticed a gray-and-white bird looking in through the glass side doors. It was a mockingbird—I recognized it from the Texas state bird coloring pages we'd had in elementary school. They weren't much fun to color, especially if you'd just opened a brand-new box of crayons.

The mockingbird glanced up at me, hopped a few steps down the sidewalk, then turned back, like it wanted me to follow. Declan was nowhere in sight. I'd make it quick, then come back for him. Outside, the bird looked back again from the edge of the sidewalk. It took off with a sharp *cheep-cheep*. I followed it to a cedar tree behind the store.

When the bird sang again, it sounded like it was calling my name. *Ni-na, Ni-na, Ni-na. See it? See it?*

On a lower branch, another mockingbird sat on a

nest of twigs. Moss peeked through the twigs and over the sides of the nest. "Yeah, I do see it!" I said. "Do y'all have eggs in there?"

The bird didn't say anything else, just hopped down and perched behind the nest.

"I'll take that as a yes." After looking around to make sure no one saw me talking to a bird, I added, "Thanks for showing me. Nice meeting you."

Back inside the store, I still saw no sign of Declan. He must've gone outside. But out in the parking lot, a different car was parked where our minivan had been. I stepped back inside to make sure this wasn't the wrong exit. No, there was the fountain drink station. This was the right set of doors.

I jogged around the store, looking up and down the aisles. Maybe my parents had forgotten something for the twins. That had to be it.

No one was shopping in the baby aisle. The minivan wasn't near any of the exits, or anywhere else in the parking lot. I patted my pockets. Empty. My phone was in the car. After another lap inside the store, I went up to the ice cream counter. Wanda had seemed nice when she gave me the lunch order.

"Back for dessert?" she said. "You didn't eat all those sandwiches yourself, did you?" She laughed. Not like Sage laughed when she was talking to those boys. Wanda laughed like she meant it.

"I think my family forgot me?" It came out like a question. Even though that had to be what happened, it was too ridiculous to believe.

Wanda looked around, like maybe my family was standing there and I hadn't noticed them. She set aside her ice cream scoop and said, "You mean like they left you here?"

I nodded. After getting another worker to take her place, Wanda stepped through the little half door next to the ice cream counter and put a hand on my shoulder. "Everything's going to be just fine," she said. I looked up and blinked a few times, hoping Wanda didn't notice I was trying not to cry. She led me to a break room and said, "Wait right here," then went to find her manager.

Wanda returned after a few minutes. "Your folks called to make sure you were okay," she said. "They're headed back. Bet they came to a screeching halt on the highway when they realized you weren't with them! How about some ice cream? What's your favorite flavor of Blue Bell?"

"Cookies 'n' cream is the best."

Wanda pointed at me and said, "Smart girl. Be right back with a cone."

Sometimes at home we had cookies 'n' cream in the freezer, but I could never get to it before Declan tunneled through the carton to dig out the best chunks. The scoop Wanda gave me was full of cookies. She'd brought a cone for herself, too, and sat with me in the break room while we waited for my family.

"Such a big store," Wanda said. "People start looking around and lose track of time—and each other!" She was probably trying to make me feel better about getting left behind. I hadn't planned to tell anyone about the mockingbird. Most people would think it was weird. But I felt safe telling Wanda.

"That isn't how we lost track of each other." I told her all about the mockingbird—going outside to follow him down the sidewalk and to the tree, where he showed me his nest and sang my name.

Wanda's eyes widened. "Mockingbirds usually dive-bomb anyone who comes near their nests. They're territorial." She leaned in like she was telling me a secret. "But I think animals know who the good people are. That bird trusted you."

I could've stayed there all day, talking to Wanda in the break room. She seemed like the kind of person who'd have a cozy house. A small house, kind of old, but comfortable, maybe with a cat curled up on one end of a plaid fabric couch.

Manager Mavis came in soon, followed by Dad, who looked frantic. He wrapped me in a tight hug and told me he was sorry. So very, very sorry. "How could we have left you?" It didn't seem like he expected an answer, and I didn't give one. But I thought, "Yeah, how could you leave me?" They'd driven away, not noticing anything was wrong. Like nothing was missing from the family.

We both thanked Wanda, then walked together to the van.

Turned out it was Chloe who'd noticed I wasn't with them. Declan told me that the van was ten miles down the road when Chloe said, "Where's Nina?" At the same time, Mom was passing out the sandwiches and realized she had one extra.

Sage and Declan got in trouble for not staying with me, and Mom and Dad seemed mad at each other.

"I'm sorry," I said. They were all unwrapping their sandwiches by then. I unwrapped mine, too, even though I wasn't hungry.

"Ewww, pickles!" said Sage from the seat in front of me.

As we continued down the highway, I looked out the window and said, "A bird sang my name and showed me his nest." Maybe no one heard me, but that didn't matter. I said it again, for myself, to remember it was real.

"A bird sang my name."

Chapter 2

After that day at Buc-ee's, I listened and looked for birds everywhere. The birding apps I'd added to my phone had pictures of every bird, so I could match them with pictures I took. The best apps recognized birdsong, too. If I turned on the recording as soon as I heard a song, the app showed me who was singing. In the mornings, when birds were busiest, a long list of birds appeared under a sound graph. The apps also had checklists to keep track of sightings. I checked off cardinals, blue jays, house sparrows, and a few others right away, but a couple of weeks had passed since I'd spotted something new. Mom let me order a cheap trail cam to set up in different areas of the yard at night. First thing every morning, I'd check out what images it had captured of birds who woke up before I did. Sage thought the squirrels and raccoons who visited our bird feeders were cute, even though they ate all the food before the birds could get to it.

One Friday after school, I stopped at home just long enough to grab a quick snack before running back out to look for birds. Declan was in the driveway, practicing his basketball shots.

"Hey, Birdbrain," he said.

"Birds are actually really smart," I said.

He shook his head and went back to throwing his basketball.

My favorite tree was an old oak a few streets away from home, thick with leaves, perfect to hide in while watching for birds. Its lowest branch, wide as a park bench, practically invited me to hop on. I didn't pick that tree just because it grew across from my friend's house. Well, not my friend, really. Iris wouldn't call us that. But maybe we *could* be friends, if we had a chance to talk again. We used to go to the same school, but not anymore. That might have been my fault.

From my perch in the tree, I sat still and listened to a birdcall. I liked to guess who was singing before spotting the bird or checking the app. While still listening to the birdsong, I looked for a flicker of movement. This one sounded like a blue jay—an annoyed blue jay. Maybe it wasn't fair to think that. For all I knew, blue jays sounded like that when they were happy.

Leaves rustled on a tree next to me, even though I didn't feel any wind. There—a blue jay. I was right.

At the sound of laughter, I turned my attention from the blue jay to a pair of girls walking down the sidewalk. They looked maybe ten or eleven. Their voices carried to the tree, but not enough for me to overhear what they said. I wondered what one girl had said to make the other laugh. Maybe she told a joke. Not the kind that makes fun of someone, but a joke that makes everyone laugh together. Or maybe it wasn't a joke at all. Just a funny story.

I made up a story about how they became friends. Their parents knew each other, and they used to meet for playdates at the park, or to go out for ice cream. The girls were older now but still liked each other. It just worked out that way. They'd laugh about things they'd done when they were little kids. They never got to the point where one of them said the other was acting like a baby and that they'd found other friends to hang out with. Or maybe they were new friends. They met at school and discovered they liked the same things. Ballet or kittens or comic books.

I pointed my phone at the girls, pretending I had an app that would ID them for me. Not just their names, but who they really were. What kinds of things they liked, how they decided to hang out with someone, what it would take to be their friend.

Unlike with my birding apps, I couldn't check any of that. It was all a mystery. Other people somehow knew how to make friends, like they'd all been handed an instruction manual one day when I was absent.

I'd climbed partway down the tree when the front door opened at Iris's house. She and her older brother walked out. I tried to catch what they were saying to each other. The problem wasn't that they were too far away for me to hear them, but that they used sign language because Iris was Deaf. I'd learned some, but not enough to understand their conversation.

I'd tried to be friends with Iris before but made a big mess of things. Every time I sat in that tree, I imagined what I'd say to her. Maybe I'd be heading home, then stop to say, "Oh, hi!" like it was a surprise to see her. The conversation could start out that way, before I'd bring up a bird fact I was hanging on to—the best bird fact ever. I hadn't told anyone else about it. It was a whale fact, too. Iris would like that part, so I'd start there, signing *whale* first to grab her attention. Then I'd tell her the rest of it, and we'd be on our way to being friends.

But whenever I thought about jumping down from the tree to talk to her, the branches held me in place. Making up a conversation between us, one where Iris was happy to see me, was easier. We'd talk about how school was going, and I'd ask if I was the reason she transferred schools. *Is it because I was annoying?* Then she'd say, *No, of course not. You weren't annoying at all.* Then I'd point out some birds and tell her about them.

Maybe it would go that way if I jumped down from the tree. Or maybe one look at Iris's face would show me that she didn't want to talk to me. Even worse, she might pretend not to see me at all.

Iris and her brother got into his truck and backed out of the driveway. I stayed hidden in the branches until they were out of sight.

Chapter 3

Sage was on the couch typing on her laptop when I got home, while Declan sat on the floor watching something on his tablet. I was about to head up to my room when Sage said, "Nina, wait."

"What?"

She closed her laptop and patted the place next to her on the couch. After I sat down, she said, "I learned a bird fact today. It's about bird brains."

"Nina's an expert in that," said Declan.

I ignored him and said, "Okay. I probably know about it already, though."

"Have you heard of zugunruhe?"

"Zoo what?" I asked.

"It's a German word. Zoo-gun-roo. It's what tells birds it's time to migrate. Something in their brains tells them it's time to go. Maybe they don't even know where that is yet. They'll figure it out on the way. But they feel pulled to leave, and they do. They just go. You think people have something like that, too?"

Sage stared out the window. It didn't seem like she was waiting for an answer. "Part of our brain is the same as a bird's, right?" she continued. "It's in there somewhere, telling us that we need to leave, that there's somewhere else we're supposed to be."

Sage looked like she wanted to fly away then, but why? Her life was perfect. That summer she'd have an internship at a senator's office, which meant she'd be working there for free. That didn't make sense to me, but Mom and Dad said it would be an excellent addition to Sage's college applications. I figured Sage was happy about it, too.

Declan stood up and said, "Wait, I'm feeling it. Something's pulling me . . . to the kitchen. It's the cookies 'n' cream!"

"He's going to scoop out all the cookie chunks," I said.

"You could go, you know," said Sage.

"To the kitchen?"

"I mean somewhere else. For the summer. You don't have to stay here and do all the things Mom signed you up for. Isn't there, like, I don't know, a bird camp or something? What about Aunt Audrey's camp? It looks like a fun place, from the pictures she posts. There must be something else out there for you, somewhere else you're supposed to be."

I hadn't thought of that. Mom liked to fill our summers with activities. She'd registered me for a couple of things and would let me choose some others, but I hadn't picked anything yet. If I didn't take care of that soon, she'd decide for me. One of the brochures she'd set out for me to look at was a weeklong floral-arranging day camp. Nothing against flowers, but I didn't want to spend a week of my summer arranging them.

In my room later, I looked up the word Sage told me about. It came up pretty quickly, even though I didn't know how to spell it. Zugunruhe. The article said that birds get restless when it was time to migrate. It even happens to birds that don't or can't migrate, like if they're in captivity. They'll wander around and flap their wings like they're getting ready to take off. Some try to fly away, hitting the bars of their cage. That was too sad to read about, so I closed the article.

But maybe Sage had a point.

My aunt Audrey ran a camp in a town called Bee Holler, about a two-hour drive from home. She used to invite us to spend some of our summer breaks there. I think she gave up on asking because my parents would answer, "Yeah, maybe!" and never take her up on it.

I asked Mom about going there for the summer, and she said she'd talk to Dad about it. Sometimes that meant they'd talk about it and then tell me no anyway.

That evening I listened outside the downstairs bathroom while Mom and Dad gave the twins a bath. Unfortunately, Chloe's and Aiden's voices were louder than our parents'. Between that and the splashing, only snippets of the conversation made it through the door.

". . . something she's good at," Dad said.

"But birds . . . ?" said Mom. ". . . living in the woods . . . the influence we want . . . ?"

They were probably discussing how bird-watching would look on a college application, even though that was years away for me. Maybe it'd be a good idea to look up birding scholarships, just in case.

Mom said something about Aunt Audrey, but I couldn't hear what.

Declan walked into the kitchen then, backing up a step when he noticed me in the hallway.

He started to speak, so I held a finger to my lips. Knowing Declan, he was probably about to ask what I was doing, even though it was obvious: listening to Mom and Dad through the bathroom door. Trying to, anyway. No telling which version of Declan I'd get—the one who'd yell out, "Hey, Nina!" or the nice one who'd understand that this was important. I gave him my best "Please don't ruin this for me" look. He glanced from me to the closed bathroom door. Then he shook his head, like I was being a weird birdbrain. But he did walk away.

Mom and Dad came into my room later as I was getting ready for bed. Mom sighed and said, "Okay. We've talked it over, and we decided you can go to camp. I called Audrey about it, too, and she said she'd love to have you there. You'll stay in the spare bedroom at her cabin."

"Really? I can go?"

"Yes," said Mom. "Audrey is—"

"An odd duck," said Dad. "Hey, maybe you'll like that! You know, because of the bird thing."

"I was going to say 'Audrey is Audrey,'" said Mom. "But she's family. She'll take care of you."

I jumped up and gave them each a hug. "Thank you!"

They both laughed. "You're welcome," said Mom. "But look, we want you to participate in the activities, not just sleep and read and look for birds."

"I will. Do stuff, I mean. Camp stuff."

"And make an effort to make friends with the other girls," she added.

I nodded but didn't say anything. I always made an effort.

Dad tousled my hair and said, "You're sure you want to go, kid? We're going to miss you around here."

Parents have to say that kind of thing. I didn't remind

him that they'd driven away from Buc-ee's without me. "I'm sure. I'll miss you, too."

Sage looked happy for me when we told her and Declan about camp. "I'll fill your bird feeders for you," she said.

"Thanks. I might not stay all summer. Mom said I could come home if I don't like it."

"You'll like it," she said. "Even if you think you don't at first, try to stick it out."

"It'll be weird around here without you," said Declan. "I mean, even weirder than when you're here."

Mom said that was Declan's way of saying he'd miss me. Declan and I both laughed at that, but Mom didn't look like she was trying to make a joke. She looked like she believed it.

Chapter 4

During the next two weeks, Mom shopped like I'd be spending a year on a desert island. She packed my suitcase with enough bug spray and sunblock to last the rest of my life. I wouldn't have been surprised to find a can of bear spray in there. The inside pocket held stationery and stamps. Even though I'd be able to call home, Mom wanted me to write letters, too.

Finally, my life at camp was about to start. Both Mom and Dad wanted to take me, so the three of us packed up the minivan and headed to Bee Holler. We'd been on the road for almost two hours when Mom said we should make a Buc-ee's stop.

"We'll be at the camp soon," said Dad.

"Exactly," said Mom. "No telling how long the tour will take. You think I'm trusting the camp bathrooms?

For all we know, they hand you a shovel so you can dig your own."

Dad laughed. "I'm sure it's not like that. The staff will dig a hole for you."

Mom gave him a little smack to the upper arm, and Dad laughed again. From where I sat in the back seat, I could see the hint of a smile at the corner of Mom's mouth, even though she was trying to look mad.

Dad took the next exit, right after the billboard of the Buc-ee's beaver pointing the way.

We turned onto a red dirt road next to a faded wooden Camp Bee Holler sign. Aunt Audrey had told us to meet her at the camp office, close to the front gate.

The office building looked like a small log cabin. On the wall next to the screen door, a wooden sign spelled out OFFICE in black letters. Three steps led up to the front porch.

Audrey stepped out of the office even before we got out of the car, like she couldn't wait for our visit to start. Or maybe she just wanted to be outdoors. She always looked out of place indoors, as if someone had planted an oak tree in the living room.

Audrey smiled and clasped her hands together. She wore her regular uniform of khaki shorts and a Camp Bee Holler T-shirt. She must have had a closet full of those shirts—I never saw her wear anything else. Her light brown ponytail was threaded through the hole in the back of her baseball cap.

Audrey bounded down the stairs to greet me, then wrapped me in a hug. "You're really here."

I smiled and said, "I really am."

She took a step back and looked at me, like she could hardly believe it.

She hugged my dad next and said, "Great to see you, Tom."

"You too," said Dad.

When she turned to my mom, they moved toward each other and back a little, like they were afraid they'd bump heads, trying to figure out which way they'd fit together. It reminded me of that awkward moment at a school dance when the music switched from a fast song to a slow one.

They both giggled a little, then hugged. "Thanks so much for bringing her," said Audrey.

"Of course," said Mom, as if it had never been a question. "Looking forward to seeing the place."

Even though we'd visited Audrey before, we hadn't explored much of the camp. We'd usually hang around her cabin, and I'd walk some of the trails with Sage and Declan. Since I'd be staying there this time, Mom wanted a tour. Hopefully she wouldn't see anything that would make her change her mind. She had said earlier that if she saw anything of concern on the tour, we'd make it just a short visit, and I'd be going back home.

"Let's start with the office," said Audrey. "Then I'll grab my keys, and we'll tour the rest of camp on that sweet ride." She pointed to a vehicle that looked kind of like a golf cart, but with wider tires and a camouflage paint job.

We followed her into the office cabin, a boxy room with a desk and a computer. A metal file cabinet stood in one corner. Framed watercolor paintings sat on the file cabinet and the desk. I wasn't sure what the paintings were supposed to be. One looked kind of like a colorful dog and another looked like a forest. A messy forest. Broken pieces of pottery sat across a windowsill.

"You can help out in here sometimes, like with registration and answering the phone," Audrey said. Camp wouldn't start for another week. Until then, I'd help the staff, which I didn't mind. We'd have the place to ourselves for a while, before all the campers arrived.

"I know you'll want to spend time outdoors, too," Audrey continued, "but you'll welcome the AC."

I nodded. It wasn't even noon yet, but it was hot and humid outside.

"I don't know how the campers don't get heatstroke," said Mom.

"They have free time built into every day," said Audrey, "which they can spend in their cabins or in the water, if they want. Some activities take place in buildings with AC." She showed us the rest of the office, which took about two seconds, since the only other things to see were the half bathroom and small kitchen. Audrey grabbed a set of keys from her desk and said, "Now for the rest of this place."

I took a deep breath and glanced at Audrey before climbing into the back seat of the camo golf cart. She had to know how important this tour was, but she didn't look worried. Either she was good at hiding it or she thought everything would be okay. Still, even if things looked fine to everyone else, Mom could always find something wrong.

As we toured the camp, I checked Mom's expression for signs of trouble. She looked worried, but I couldn't tell if that was because she didn't want to leave me there all summer or because she saw something she didn't like.

Audrey drove up next to the swimming pool, which was surrounded by a chain-link fence.

"Looks nice and clean," said Mom.

"Not bad since we cleared out the alligators," said Audrey.

"Ha-ha," said Mom dryly. "Lifeguards will be on duty, right?"

"Here and at the lake," Audrey answered. "I'll take you there now."

Audrey also showed us the activity stations, like the arts and crafts cabin and the archery field. I probably wouldn't be doing any of that. Especially not art, since that wasn't my thing. I'd learned that a few years earlier, on day one of a weeklong art day camp. But that was okay. I was at summer camp now, where I'd get to do all the birding I wanted. The biggest building was the dining lodge, where we'd have all our meals.

Audrey pulled up next to the office when the tour was over, and Dad said, "Looks like a great place."

Mom gave a small nod and said, "Yes, it's nice. Too much"—she waved a hand—"you know, outdoors for me, but if you like that kind of thing . . ."

"You know I do," said Audrey.

"Yeah, we know." Mom took a deep breath, then asked me, "You're sure you want to stay?"

"I'm sure."

She gave me a tight hug and said, "Call me and let me know how you're doing. And write letters. If you decide you want to come home, we can come pick you up."

"I'll be okay," I said.

After she let go, she added, "All right. Be sure to do what Aunt Audrey tells you, and remember to participate in camp."

Audrey put a hand on my shoulder. "She'll do great."

Dad hugged me next. "Be good, kiddo. We love you."

"Love you, too."

They both said their goodbyes to Audrey, then headed to the van.

"Mom?" I called.

She turned around, looking hopeful, like maybe she was waiting for me to say "Never mind, I'll go back home with you."

"Thanks for letting me stay," I said.

She nodded and waved, then got into the van with Dad.

After they drove away, Audrey pointed to the golf cart and said, "Hop in, I'll show you my favorite place."

Chapter 5

"We'll stop at home first to drop off your bag," said Audrey. "And we'll switch vehicles."

I liked the way she called the cabin home. She didn't call it the cabin or her house. For the summer, Audrey's cabin would be my home, too. She parked next to an open-top Jeep dusted with red dirt. "We'll be taking that," she said. I climbed into the passenger seat while Audrey wheeled my suitcase into the cabin.

When she came back to the Jeep, she handed me a new Camp Bee Holler cap. "Here, this will keep the sun off your face."

I gathered my hair and pulled it through the hole in the back of the cap, making a shorter and darker brown ponytail than Audrey's. We coated ourselves using a can of bug spray from the Jeep's cup holder; then Audrey drove us down the road and through an open gate. The road sloped down a small hill, where we parked on a bent-down patch of reeds as wide as the Jeep. Audrey grabbed a faded blue plaid blanket and a canvas tote bag from the back seat, then led me down a faint path to a strip of shoreline at the edge of the marsh. The dirt here was dark brown instead of the rust-red of the camp trails.

"I guess you didn't want to include this on the tour?"

Audrey swatted a mosquito off my arm. "Didn't want your mom to worry about what's lurking in the marsh."

I scanned the surface of the dark water, rippled with the touches of bugs and fish.

"But I love wondering about all the life out there we can't see," said Audrey. "This is my favorite place to sit and enjoy the quiet when I want to get away from everything."

The woods and the lake were prettier, but Audrey loved the marsh, with its murky water and clumps of grass. Maybe that was unusual, but Audrey didn't seem weird to me. I still didn't see why my parents had a problem with her.

"Check out the bird over there." Audrey pointed to our right, where a large white bird waded in the marsh.

"How'd you spot that, so far away?" I asked.

"Just used to noticing things here, I guess." Audrey took a black leather case from the tote bag, unsnapped it, and pulled out a pair of binoculars. We took turns passing them back and forth. Through the binoculars, the bird seemed close enough for me to touch its feathers and its yellow-orange dagger of a beak.

"Some kind of heron, right?" I asked. "Maybe an egret?" I took out my phone to check. Audrey touched my arm. "Wait. This is a good chance to get used to not using your phone."

Mom had mentioned when we were packing that campers weren't allowed to have phones. I could bring mine but had to keep it put away. It had sounded okay at the time, but somehow it hadn't hit me that I wouldn't have my birding apps.

"How am I supposed to identify birds without my phone?"

"People were birding long before phones were around." She reached into the tote bag again, then handed me a small notebook. Line drawings of birds decorated the light blue cover. "You can keep track of the birds you see in here, and make some quick sketches to help you ID them later."

"Sketches?" I flipped through the book. Writing things down would be okay, but I didn't want to mess up the blank pages with my drawings.

"You don't have to be good at it," said Audrey, like she could hear what I was thinking. "Just sketch something you notice about the bird, like the shape of a beak or a wing. Add some notes about the colors, or what its song is like. You can use my computer or your phone at night to ID what you saw. You probably know more than you think you do. It will sharpen your skills."

That sounded like a lot more work than uploading a photo to my bird apps.

"But what if I'm wrong?"

"Who's going to complain, the birds?" said Audrey. "You can borrow my binoculars, too."

"Really?" They felt like nice binoculars, heavy, with a padded neck strap.

"Really. I don't use them often, so they sit in a drawer most of the time." She showed me how to pull up the sides to adjust the position and how to turn the black dial to focus.

"Now, back to that bird," she said. "I'll help you narrow it down. We do have a lot of big white birds in the marsh. The ibis, for one, but they're rounder than this bird, like white footballs with beaks. Little blue herons have white feathers their first year, so they look a lot like great egrets. Getting a view of the legs would help—little blue herons have green legs."

"Can't see much of the legs yet, with the water and plants hiding them," I said.

"Oh, and the herons' neck feathers are kind of shaggy."

I peered through the binoculars at the bird, adjusting the dial for a better view. "This one has a smooth neck."

I kept my eyes on its legs as it waded closer. "There they are—black legs. A great egret."

"You got it!" said Audrey. "Oh, and the little blue heron has a gray-and-black beak."

I laughed. "That would've been a good hint!"

"Hey, I didn't want to make it too easy for you."

Now I had a new bird to add to my list of sightings. I still wanted to reach for my phone to make sure we were right, but it did feel good to ID the egret just by looking at it, even with Audrey helping me. Maybe the marsh wasn't so boring. "Can we come back here sometime?"

"Sure, just don't come by yourself. I have to protect you from the marsh monsters. *Rawr!*" She snapped at my knee with her clawed hand. "Come on, I'll show you the trading post. We can taste test the ice cream bars."

Dad was right about one thing—I really did like Audrey. Maybe that made me an odd duck, too.

Chapter 6

I'd never thought about how much work went into getting camp ready. It was a lot more than opening the
gates and letting the campers swarm in. Sometimes I
helped Audrey in the office, organizing supplies or running packages to activity stations. Or I'd work with the
ranger, Dale, hauling away brush that he cleared from
hiking trails and around buildings. He let me borrow a
pair of work gloves for that, to protect my hands from
thorns. One afternoon a big delivery of art supplies arrived, and I helped the art teacher, Sasha, organize the
colored pencils, paints, and clay into separate bins.

The day before the campers arrived, I cleaned out
the last of the cabins. Audrey said campers would track
in dirt and scatter their things around, but we wanted

everything to look nice for opening day. The cabins were small, for only four campers each, but the camp had twenty-five of them. Counselors had their own cabins, which they took care of themselves.

At each cabin, I used a broom to knock cobwebs out of the corners, then dusted the windowsills and dresser. When I was finished, I walked backward through the doorway, sweeping a pile of dirt onto the ground outside the cabin.

Before leaving the last cabin, I stopped in the doorway and looked around. The next day, campers would be moving in for the summer. I imagined someone strolling in and saying "I call the top bunk!," then tossing a duffel bag onto the bed. A few games sat on top of the dresser: Scrabble, Clue, Monopoly, card games. The girls who'd live here might play those games in the evening or on rainy days. They'd talk about their favorite activities or the worst meal from the dining lodge, things they missed about home and things they didn't miss. Sometimes they'd argue, like about who was snoring at night or leaving towels on the bathroom floor. Nothing serious. Things they'd joke about later, because they were friends.

What would they think of me?

I pictured myself sitting on the floor with the other girls, a pile of Uno cards in front of us. The girls laughed at something funny I said.

I hurried out the door before the image could evaporate.

Even with all the work to do, I found time to squeeze in some birding before dinner. Sometimes Audrey walked with me or we rode a paddleboat on the lake, and she pointed out the wildlife she spotted. She'd given me a list of animals in the area, and I couldn't believe how long it was. Bird species filled one page, divided into habitats—woods, lake, and marsh—along with what seasons they lived there. Just the warbler column took up half a page. Throughout the week I'd checked a lot of birds off my list and had put question marks next to a few others. I'd also set up my trail cam, moving it to a different tree each day. It picked up some birds I'd seen at home, like cardinals. Others, like seaside sparrows, were new to me. The only birds I didn't like seeing were cowbirds. They're like cuckoo birds—instead of raising their own chicks, they lay eggs in the nests of other birds. Their eggs hatch first, so the parents end up taking care of the cowbird or cuckoo chicks instead of their own. Whenever I saw a cowbird on the trail-cam photos, I wondered about the red-winged blackbird or sparrow nest that had an imposter egg in it, crowding out the eggs that belonged there.

The evening before opening day, I sat alone at the

edge of the dock, watching a family of ducks swim across the lake. The adult looked like a female mallard, but the bill was more black than orange, and it didn't have the white tail feathers that mallards have. I scribbled a description in my notebook: *Black bill with orange tip, dark brown and black feathers, light brown face.* My phone could tell me in a few seconds what species I was looking at, but for now I'd have to ID birds like people had done in the olden days. In the evenings, I looked through my notes and tried to find a matching bird on my phone or Audrey's laptop. I wished I could search for "What bird sounds like *trill-trill-trill*?" and get an exact match. I recognized vultures circling in the sky, but not well enough to tell whether they were turkey vultures or black vultures. Audrey reminded me that I probably knew more than I gave myself credit for, and to trust what I heard and saw. I told her I'd try, but my birding apps would make it a lot easier.

I closed my eyes to listen, enjoying the quiet for the last time before the campers arrived. The outdoors wasn't actually quiet, I'd noticed. But it wasn't the kind of noisy that a crowd of people made. This was a peaceful kind of noisy, made of birdsong, frog croaks, cricket chirps, water lapping against the dock, and wind blowing through reeds.

Soon the place would be busy with campers, yelling and laughing and splashing water with oars. I had trouble imagining it right then from the dock, but it would happen.

If only Bee Holler could stay like it was, just us staff working during the day, meeting up for meals, taking breaks to swim and bird-watch and go boating. But of course, a camp had to have campers. Audrey told me that once it started I'd be sort of half staff, half camper. Where would that new camper half fit?

Then I thought again about those cuckoos, who lay their eggs in other birds' nests. Here's the brilliant thing about cuckoo eggs: the eggshell color depends on the other birds in the area. Like if a cuckoo lives near reed warblers, her eggs are a bit greenish. That way, they match the warbler eggs, and the parents don't notice the intruder. The eggs blend in well enough, even if they're not exactly the same.

I wasn't exactly a camper, but maybe I was close enough to blend in.

Chapter 7

I was on the dock again, running late for dinner. From what I'd looked up the night before, the family on the lake were probably mottled ducks. That was why I was hanging out there—to see the duck family again. Not because I was nervous about meeting the campers. Work had kept me busy most of the day, and I hadn't met any of the other girls yet. I'd planned to, really. But when I peeked outside and saw the pack of campers, I backed away from the window and found more work to do. The office closet needed organizing anyway.

Even if I hadn't known where the dining lodge was, I could've followed the sound. So many voices talking or shouting at once, like a pep rally. One group cheered, "We are the Ravens, the mighty, mighty Ravens . . . ," while another group chanted over them, "Queen Bees rule! Queen Bees rule!"

The dining lodge felt like a cafeteria on the first day of school, with me, the new kid, wondering where to sit. I missed the days when I'd had a seat at the staff table, and we'd had the place to ourselves. The other staff looked so happy, like they weren't bothered by all these intruders. Maybe they were pretending because that was their job.

Aunt Audrey bounced from table to table, chatting and getting hugs from the campers. Of course she'd know a lot of them, but I hadn't thought of that before.

The cook, Estelle, saw me hovering at the kitchen entrance, trying to decide between going in as usual or grabbing a tray at the serving line like the campers.

"Doing okay, sweetie?" Estelle asked.

"Yes, I'm okay. Need help with anything?" Staff were zipping all around the kitchen. I didn't know where I'd go or how to help, but I'd feel more comfortable in there. Something always needed chopping or cleaning up. Hot water filled the sink, ready for washing the dinner trays. Steam billowed out in a cloud, big enough for me to hide in.

Estelle smiled but waved me away. "No, go on and get your dinner. You can finally sit with the other campers instead of us old people!"

"I like the old people," I mumbled. During our last staff dinner, we made build-your-own mini pizzas. Some of the topping choices were things I'd never have thought of putting on a pizza. "Try the figs and caramelized onions," Estelle had told me, "and thank me later." It turned out to be my favorite meal of the week.

After I got my tray of chicken and dumplings, the dining lodge somehow looked even more crowded. The campers were multiplying. Maybe I could slip out the side door and eat dinner in the cabin.

A waving hand drew my attention away from the door. A Black girl with glasses and her hair in a bun motioned me over to her table. After another glance at the door, I took the empty seat across from her.

"I'm Georgie," she said. "Are you new here, too? You look lost."

"No. Well, kind of." I did feel lost, but I didn't like that it was obvious. "I'm Nina. I guess I am new, but I'm not officially a camper. Audrey's my aunt. I've been here for a week, but I haven't been to camp before. I'll just be here a few more days." I hadn't planned to say that before it came out of my mouth. But Mom did say I could go home early if I wanted to, and camp already felt too crowded for me. This place belonged to the campers—I was the intruder.

"Seems like we're the only new ones here," said a blond girl next to me, "other than the ten-year-olds.

We're the only old campers who are new." The ten-year-olds were the youngest ones at camp, and the "old" group included the thirteen- and fourteen-year-olds.

Georgie pointed her fork at the blond girl and said, "This is Emma, by the way."

"Oh right, sorry. We're in a cabin together, with Ant." Emma pointed under the table.

"Ant?"

"Yeah, here she comes," said Georgie.

A girl with tan skin and long black hair emerged from under the table. She held up her palm, where a huge black beetle sat. A sound like *meep* squeaked out of Emma's mouth.

"Look at this cute little fella," said Ant. "So glad no one stepped on him."

Georgie leaned away from her and said, "Yeah, adorable. What is it?"

"It's a stag beetle." Ant turned her palm so the light reflected off the bug. "Notice how it's not totally black, but a little blue or purplish in the light. Anyway, I'd better get him outside." She weaved around other campers as she made her way to the side door.

When she came back to the table, I said, "Your name is Ant?"

"I like ants." She said it like a warning not to ask again.

"We're sort of the leftover cabin," said Emma. She

leaned closer and said, "Seems like everyone else already knows each other, right?"

The tables around us were full of laughing and chattering campers. "Like they're all catching up with old friends," I said.

"There must be others who've never been here before, right?" said Georgie.

"Maybe," said Ant. "But most people sign up with a friend so they at least know someone when they get here."

"We just came on our own," said Emma.

"Well, now we know each other, right?" said Georgie.

"Right," I said.

"Audrey told us to choose a name for our cabin," said Emma, "so we came up with the Oddballs."

"Because of the odd number," said Ant. "Three of us instead of four."

"I thought it was because we're kind of weird," said Emma.

"That, too," said Ant.

A bell signaled the end of dinner. As we put away our trays, some girls broke into song: "Campfire, campfire, it's campfire time!" Were they going to have a song for everything?

The sun was just starting to set when we walked to the opening-day campfire.

"Hey, thanks for inviting me to sit with you," I said to Georgie. "Glad you noticed I looked lost."

"Me too," she said.

Estelle was already at the campfire area when we got there, next to two metal carts full of foil trays and stacks of bowls. A blue cooler sat on the ground in front of the carts.

"Want to help with the cobbler?" Estelle asked when she saw me. "Most of my staff is still cleaning up the kitchen."

I wondered if she actually needed help or just knew I wanted something to do. Either way was fine with me. "Thanks, Estelle. I mean, sure, I'll help."

"Audrey will announce when it's time to pass it out. For now, scoop the ice cream onto the cobbler after I put it into the bowls. If she keeps her introduction short, we won't end up with ice cream soup."

"Yeah, it's not exactly campfire weather," I said. The campfire was mostly hot coals instead of burning flames, but it still added waves of heat to the already hot evening.

"The fire keeps the bugs away, though," said Estelle. "Most of them."

Estelle set bowls of peach cobbler on the tray for me to top with vanilla Blue Bell; then one of the counselors set the bowls on a folding table. Campers filled the rows of logs arranged like benches in front of the fire, then cheered when Aunt Audrey walked up and welcomed everyone to Camp Bee Holler.

Audrey introduced herself by saying, "For those who don't know me yet, I'm Audrey, the camp director. Most people here call me Aunt Audrey." I hadn't known that the campers called her that. She continued, "For some of you, it's your first time here—the first of many, we hope—but most of you have been to Bee Holler before. A lot of you started coming when you were ten years old, and now you're here as fourteen-year-olds, campers for the last time. I hope you'll stay on with us as counselors in the future. We've loved seeing you grow up over the years."

"Or not grow up!" a blond girl in the front row called out.

Audrey laughed along with the campers. "Right, or not grow up, Cecilia. And the rest of you joining us again—let's hear from you if you're a returning camper."

Loud applause and cheers broke out. Audrey raised one hand, which must have been a "get quiet" signal since the noise died down.

"I asked that for a couple of reasons," Audrey said. "One, if you're a first-time camper, you'll make plenty of friends who'll help you out if you're not sure where to go or what activity to choose. You have your counselors, of course, but you also have other campers to turn to.

Which brings me to my second point—it says a lot about this place that we have so many campers who come back every year. There's nowhere else I'd rather be, and I love getting to share this place with you."

One of the counselors, Britt, slapped her own arm and said, "Share the bugs, you mean."

"You caught me," said Audrey. "Yes, the mosquitoes have more meals to choose from now. Seriously, we're like a family here, and we help each other out. And speaking of family—"

I stopped mid-scoop and looked up.

"—there's someone here who's been calling me Aunt Audrey for a lot longer than anyone else." Audrey waved toward me, and everyone turned my direction. "I'm so happy to have my niece with us this summer. Everyone say hi to Nina."

"Hi, Nina!" the group called out.

I wiped my hand on the side of my shorts, as if I had to get rid of the ice cream stickiness, then waved to the crowd. "Hi, um, everyone." For a second, I worried I'd have to give a speech, but Audrey picked it up again.

"Nina's been helping the staff get ready for your arrival, and now she'll have some fun, too, participating in camp activities."

"Starting now, with ghost stories!" someone shouted.

After more cheering, Audrey said, "Okay, who's ready for cobbler and story time?"

Some of the staff picked up cobbler bowls to pass out while Britt started the ghost stories. I found an empty spot next to Emma, and she moved closer to Georgie and Ant to make room for me.

Britt told a couple of ghost stories that started out spooky and suspenseful but ended in a joke. One was about a bloody-fingered ghost who asked for a Band-Aid, and another was about a monster who chased a camper through the woods, just to say "Tag, you're it!" when he caught her. I couldn't help laughing, even though the stories were kind of dumb.

"Tell the Josephine story!" called Cecilia. Some other girls clapped and chanted, "Jo-se-phine! Jo-se-phine!"

Britt pointed to the back row and said, "Mindy tells that one best."

Emma leaned over to me and whispered, "Who's Josephine?"

I shrugged. "Guess we'll find out."

Mindy walked up to the campfire and waved at the crowd to quiet down. "You're sure you want to hear this?" she asked.

Shouts of "Yes!" and "Come on, Mindy!" came from the audience.

"Okay, but no crawling into your counselors' cabins if you're scared in the middle of the night. You've been warned."

After more encouragement from the crowd, Mindy

started the story. "It was a hundred years ago, right here at this camp. Yes, the camp has been around that long."

"I wasn't running it then, in case anyone's wondering," Audrey chimed in.

That brought some giggles from the campers, and Mindy continued, "A camper named Josephine got sick soon after she arrived. No, it wasn't because of Estelle's cooking. Turned out it was TB—tuberculosis. This was back when diseases were harder to treat. They worried it might spread around camp. Flu outbreaks had killed a lot of people. Josephine was quarantined in the infirmary. Not the infirmary we have now, so don't worry if you have to visit the nurse here. Anyway, Josephine's parents were coming to pick her up, but they lived far away. So she had to stay alone in the infirmary cabin, waiting and waiting. The nurse brought her meals and took care of her the best she could. Other than that, all Josephine had to keep her company were the marsh animals she could see from her window. When the nurse told Josephine she was sorry she had to stay there alone, Josephine said, 'But I'm not alone. The animals are here. They know I need them.' The nurse thought she'd been hallucinating because of the high fever. Well, Josephine's parents finally arrived, but they were too late. She was already gone. Later, when the nurse was cleaning out the infirmary, she found drawings of the marsh animals on the wall next to Josephine's bed. She'd carved them with her pocketknife—birds, frogs, even bugs. So maybe they really had kept her company. After that, whenever someone went to the infirmary, they didn't stay long. They always felt a chill—"

"I wouldn't mind feeling a chill about now," said Estelle. She was still at the metal cart, scooping out cobbler for those who wanted seconds. I laughed. I'd been so lost in the story, imagining Josephine lying in that infirmary alone, watching the marsh animals while she waited for her parents to come. Estelle's joke reminded me that we were at camp, sitting on logs and listening to stories in front of a fire.

"That does sound good right now, Estelle," said Mindy. "But this wasn't a chill like a cool breeze. People who visited the infirmary felt the kind of chill that makes the hair on the back of your neck stand on end."

Emma shivered next to me, then giggled. I rubbed my arms, feeling the prickle of hair standing up.

"The kind of chill that warns you that something's wrong. Some people said they heard moaning, like Josephine was still battling her fever and waiting for her parents. Others said they felt someone standing next to them, but when they turned to look, no one was there. No one they could see, anyway. Over the years, the marsh grew closer and closer to the infirmary, until the people had to abandon that part of camp. It belongs to Josephine and her animal friends now. Water makes ghosts stronger, did you know that? A few people who ventured out there at night said they saw a figure dressed in white drifting over the marsh. It must be Josephine, still guarding the animals who kept her company until the end."

Now it was my turn to shiver.

We all applauded as Mindy took a bow at the end of her story.

Ant leaned over and said, "That was a good one."

"Yeah, I wonder if it's true," said Emma.

"The Josephine part, or the ghost part?" asked Georgie.

"Both," said Emma.

We put our cobbler dishes onto the cart to be wheeled back to the kitchen. Aunt Audrey told me she'd hang around for a while to make sure the campfire was completely out—any embers could start a fire overnight. "Go ahead to the cabin and I'll see you there pretty soon," she told me.

"Umm, okay," I said.

Emma said, "Want us to walk with you?"

"Our cabin is on the way," added Georgie.

I laughed. I'd planned to start down the trail like I didn't mind, but the Oddballs could tell I didn't want to walk in the dark by myself. It was kind of silly—the cabin wasn't that far, plus I had my flashlight and probably wouldn't meet any ghosts along the way—but the woods seemed darker and scarier after Josephine's story.

"Come on," said Ant, "we'll protect you." She jumped onto the trail in a fighting stance, fists up.

"You think you're going to punch a ghost?" said Emma. "Your hands would go right through them."

"Oh, right," said Ant. "You first." She nudged us along, like we were her protective wall.

When we made it safely to Audrey's front porch, I asked, "Which cabin is yours?"

Emma pointed down the trail. "Number twenty-five."

"Yeah, stop by sometime if you want," said Georgie.

"Okay. Thanks for walking me back. I was a little creeped out."

As they left, Ant called, "Don't worry, I'm sure Josephine won't be tapping on your window tonight or anything." After a spooky laugh, she added, "Sweet dreams!"

I wondered if Georgie meant it about me visiting their cabin. People said things like that to be polite. She seemed to really mean it, though. Maybe I would stop by sometime.

The next day, I helped Audrey in the office, between going to activities with the campers. My absolute favorite activity was the blob, which was like an inflatable mountain on the lake. We climbed onto it and jumped into the water, over and over again. Sometimes the counselors jumped onto the blob together, catapulting us off.

While we sat on the dock, still laughing and drying off, a counselor named Libby pointed at a flock of birds in the sky. "Ooh, look," she said. "Notice how they make different shapes."

The birds flew together, forming shapes in the sky. Some of the girls called out what the shapes looked like, as if we were watching clouds, but the birds changed a lot faster than clouds did. As soon as someone said, "Look, it's a race car!" the flock morphed into a tree or a dog or a picnic basket.

"It's a hamburger!" one girl said when the birds rearranged themselves again.

"Great, now I'm hungry," said a girl named Vivienne.

Libby laughed and asked, "Who knows what birds those are?"

No one chimed in, so I shouted, "Starlings!"

"That's right!" said Libby. "They stay together by keeping an eye on the birds around them. If they start to drift away from the flock, they use the position of the birds next to them to adjust."

Somehow I'd missed that when I'd read about starlings. I hadn't thought about how they stayed together so well.

"That's so cool!" one girl said.

I was bursting to tell everyone all about them. "They're actually an invasive species, from Europe," I said. "They didn't fly all the way over from there. People brought them. They released a hundred of them in Central Park in New York a long time ago. One thing I read said the group who released them wanted every bird from Shakespeare's plays to live here in the United States. Most didn't make it, but the starlings and house sparrows did." Everyone was quiet, watching me. I told myself to stop, that they'd heard enough. But sometimes when I got going, I couldn't hold back. Maybe the next thing I said would get them interested, and they'd see how fascinating it all was.

"They have really pretty feathers, if you see them up close," I continued. "Like iridescent green and purple."

"Okay, Wikipedia," said Cecilia. "We get it."

The laughter died down after a stern look from Libby, aimed at Cecilia.

"Sorry," Cecilia mumbled.

"It's okay," I said, even though it wasn't. I didn't know what else to say, though. It felt like someone had stuck a knife into the blob and deflated all the fun.

"Thank you, Nina," said Libby. "Starlings do have a fascinating history. People didn't know back then that it's never a good idea to release a non-native species into a new location."

One of the younger girls touched my arm as we walked away from the lake. "I thought it was really interesting," she said.

"Thanks," I mumbled.

"And Wikipedia's not that bad of a nickname," said Vivienne. "I've been Farmer Viv for three years. I've accepted it now."

"Farmer Viv?" I said.

"Yeah. When I first came to camp, I was wearing a straw hat."

"That's it?"

"That's all it takes."

I liked Birdbrain better.

After that I stopped by the cabin to send a text message to Mom. *Hi Mom,* I wrote. *It's been fun here, but I'm ready to go home. Can you pick me up soon?*

Here's something else about cuckoo eggs: sometimes the parents notice a new egg that doesn't look like the others, and they throw it out of the nest. Maybe that cuckoo egg kind of looks like their own, but it's obvious it doesn't belong there.

Chapter 8

At dinner that night, Cecilia slid into an empty seat at our table. "You know about the old infirmary yet?" she asked. "We're going out there tonight."

I glanced around at the other girls, who looked as confused as I was. "As in . . . Josephine's infirmary?" Ant asked. "From the ghost story? Why?"

"It's a tradition," said Cecilia. "The older girls go out to the infirmary on the first full moon of camp—which is tonight."

"You mean it's still standing?" asked Georgie. "After a hundred years?"

Cecilia shrugged and said, "Well, barely. The floor and the walls are mostly there. A bit of a roof. Oh, and there's a wall everyone signs after they've been there.

You'll see. Every year, some campers say they can hear Josephine's ghost out there, howling."

"Maybe it's a wolf," said Emma.

The thought of meeting a wolf instead of a ghost didn't make me feel any better about this plan. It could be loons. Some of their calls sounded kind of like howling.

"There aren't any wolves here," said Georgie.

"So we're back to it being a howling ghost, then," said Ant.

"Where is the old infirmary?" Emma asked.

"In a part of camp that's closed now, near the marsh. Some of us who went out there last year will lead the way. It's not too far, just hard to find if you don't know what you're looking for."

"Nina, what do you think?" asked Ant. "Would Audrey let you stay at our cabin tonight? Then you could go with us."

No one ever asked me what I thought. It could be fun to stay with the girls in their cabin, but I didn't really want to go wandering around in the woods at night.

Cecilia's eyes grew wide and she covered her mouth. "Oh, Wikipedia! I'm so stupid! I was thinking you were a normal camper. I don't mean you're not normal, but I forgot. Anyway, you won't tell Aunt Audrey on us, right?

I promise it's safe. We go as a group and stick together. And this is my last year at camp—"

"It's okay, she's cool," said Emma. "Right, Nina?"

I thought of those starlings again, and the way they stayed together by watching the birds around them, adjusting their position to get back on course if they started to drift from the flock.

Cool Nina. That was who I'd be.

"Well, it's a tradition, right?" I said. "Let's do it."

The other girls smiled, but they looked a little nervous, too. I probably looked the same way. If we got in trouble, my mom would never let me out of her sight again. She worried enough about bug bites and snakes and germs and whatever else lurked in the woods, without knowing I'd been wandering around at night looking for a ghost in a pretty-much-standing building. It was a miracle she'd let me come to camp without covering me in Bubble Wrap first.

"Great," said Cecilia. She looked relieved that I wasn't going to snitch and ruin the adventure. "Meet on the trail in front of cabin twenty at midnight. Keep your flashlights off so the counselors won't see. Audrey's the best, but if someone breaks the rules . . ." She grimaced and sliced a finger across her throat.

"What happens if we get caught?" asked Emma.

"I don't think anyone's ever been caught going to the old infirmary, but girls have been sent home for other stuff, like setting off fireworks or trapping a squirrel to keep as a pet in the cabin. Anyway, we'll turn our flash-lights on once we're far enough down the trail."

My parents had told me I had to follow the camp rules, even though I wasn't officially a camper. I hadn't really thought about it since I hadn't planned on break-ing any rules.

After Cecilia ran off to continue spreading the news, Ant asked me, "Did she call you Wikipedia?"

I looked down at my tray of spaghetti. "Um, yeah," I said. "A joke, sort of, from the lake earlier. I didn't want to tell anyone."

"Why?" said Ant.

I wasn't sure if she meant why did Cecilia call me that or why didn't I want to tell anyone, but my answer worked either way. "It's like she was calling me a know-it-all."

Ant shrugged. "Nothing wrong with knowing stuff. Anyway, we're really doing this tonight? Going to the haunted infirmary?"

"We're probably not supposed to go out there," said Georgie.

"Maybe," said Emma. "But no one told us that the haunted infirmary is off-limits."

"Please stop calling it haunted!" said Georgie. "And no, no one specifically mentioned it, but we're not sup-posed to leave the campgrounds."

"It's probably still camp property," said Ant. "Just a part that no one's using."

"No one but the ghost," said Emma.

After a glance at Georgie, I said, "We'll be careful. We'll stick together, right?"

"Right," said Ant. "We'll check it out and come right back."

"Unless we get kidnapped," said Emma. Ant elbowed her in the side.

"We're still on the buddy system," said Ant, "even when we're breaking the rules. Anything goes wrong or looks too dangerous, we'll bail."

"Okay," said Georgie, who looked like she was warming to the plan. "The buddy system. We'll watch out for each other."

While I was packing a bag for the sleepover, Mom texted to see how I was doing. I wasn't sure what to tell her. I'd had fun at the lake, until I overdid it with the starling facts. And the girls from the Oddballs cabin were nice. But I didn't really belong. I wasn't a camper and wasn't a staffer. I was something in between, only because Audrey let me hang out there.

Doing ok, I answered. *Some girls invited me to stay in their cabin tonight, so I'm about to go over there.*

That's great! So happy you're making friends.
Think you'll want to stay longer?

I still want to come home. Can you pick me up?

Ok, if you're sure. I'll call you in the morning and
we'll figure out what day is best. Have fun tonight!

Thanks, Mom.

Audrey appeared at the doorway and said, "Ready to go? I'll walk you over there."

"I'm ready." I slung the tote bag over my shoulder. "I can go on my own, though. The Oddballs cabin isn't far."

"I know," said Audrey, "but it's dark out, and I don't want you walking around alone."

I hadn't told Audrey that I'd asked Mom to pick me up. Maybe she wouldn't mind much since she was so busy, but I didn't want to hurt her feelings.

When we got to the cabin, Audrey knocked on the door and announced, "Special delivery!"

"Audrey." I rolled my eyes but laughed, too.

Emma opened the door and said, "Welcome to Camp Oddball!"

Inside, Georgie pointed out my bed, one of the bottom bunks.

"So, how's everything going?" Audrey asked. "Having a good start to camp?"

"Yes, it's been so much fun!" said Emma.

"I'm playing basketball tomorrow," said Ant.

"Basketball?" I hadn't seen a court anywhere.

"It's one of our water sports," said Audrey.

"A lot cooler that way," said Georgie.

"Basketball?" I said again. "A water sport?"

Audrey shrugged. "Any sport is a water sport if you play it in the water. Stop by the pool tomorrow and check it out. Well, I'll leave you to your sleepover. Have fun, and you girls let me know if you need anything, okay?"

"Thanks, Aunt Audrey," the girls said.

After Audrey left, Emma said, "Okay, now what do we do until midnight?"

"Tell ghost stories?" suggested Ant.

"Going to the infirmary will be scary enough," said Georgie. "I don't need to get more scared before we leave."

I pointed to the stack of board games. "How about Monopoly?"

"Can I be the dog?" asked Georgie. "I miss my dog."

We sat on the floor with the game board between us, like I'd pictured campers doing when I cleaned the cabins. And now here I was, just like one of them. We played for about an hour, until Fiona and Libby came by.

"Time for lights-out," Fiona said.

"Aww, just look at this winning streak!" said Ant. She'd bought up most of the properties, so the rest of us had to pay her on almost every turn.

"But we're broke!" said Emma. "We can't afford rent anymore."

Ant held up fistfuls of paper money and gave an evil laugh.

"Looks like you're the winner, Ant," said Libby.

"See y'all in the morning," said Fiona on their way out.

After cleaning up the game and getting ready for bed, we still had a long wait before meeting up with the other girls.

"Now what?" Emma asked once we were all in bed with the lights off.

"I'll set an alarm in case we fall asleep," said Ant.

"Good idea," I said, even though I was too anxious to sleep.

"How about another game?" said Georgie. "Like truth or dare, but without the dares."

We laughed. "So . . . truth or truth?" said Emma.

"I never like the dares!" said Georgie. "Plus, it's kind of hard to do any dares when we're supposed to be asleep."

"Okay, who's first?" said Emma.

"You are!" said Ant. "How about . . . tell us the worst thing you got in trouble for at school."

"Okay," said Emma. "But you have to understand, I was kind of a weird kid."

"Was?" said Ant.

"Very funny," said Emma. "Weirder than I am now, I mean. Anyway, I went to detention."

"Are you skipping over why you had detention?" I asked.

"That's it, I wasn't actually assigned detention. I just went."

"Wait, you went on your own?" asked Georgie.

"Like, for fun?" said Ant.

"More like for quiet reading time, but yeah, I went on my own. I'd peeked into the detention room before, and saw that all the kids were in their own cubicles, eating lunch and reading or doing classwork. It looked so peaceful. But I didn't want to actually do anything to get in trouble. So one day when I was getting to the really good part of a new Nessie McGee mystery, I took my lunch and my book to the detention room. Have you ever tried to read in the cafeteria? It's impossible."

"Couldn't you go to the library?" asked Georgie.

"I wish, but they don't let us eat lunch in the library. The detention teacher said my name wasn't on the list, but I told her I'd just been assigned lunch detention. I left out the part about assigning it to myself. She gave me the sign-in sheet to add my name, and then I picked out a cubicle and got to finish my book."

"They didn't check with your teacher?" I asked.

"I thought they might," said Emma, "but I guess they don't bother checking, because who's going to show up to serve detention if they don't have to?"

"Just you," said Ant.

"Right, just me. I liked it so much I went the next day, with a new book, and kept going every day. It was like my own little office. Well, one day my teacher came by to drop off work for another kid and asked why I was there. I couldn't come up with an answer. That's when the detention teacher told her I'd been there every day. And I was in trouble for real."

"What happened then?" I asked.

"I had to serve detention."

I thought we'd laugh about that all night. We'd get quiet for a while, until one of us started giggling again. At some point, I must have drifted off to sleep, because when the alarm went off, it took me a minute to remember where I was. At first, I thought it was time to get ready for school. The sound of crickets outside reminded me that I was at camp. It would've been okay with me if we'd slept past the alarm. Maybe it'd be fun to see the old infirmary, but I really didn't want to hike to a maybe-haunted old building at night.

We all rolled out of bed and grabbed our flashlights, keeping them off like Cecilia had said.

Georgie picked up a can of bug spray from the dresser and said, "We'll need this." We took turns covering ourselves with the spray, then sprayed each other's backs.

"Okay, ready?" said Emma.

"Ready," I said.

Before we left, Ant stopped at the doorway and said, "Wait . . ."

I was hoping she'd say, "Never mind, let's stay in." But what she said was "Anyone have a pen?"

"Why?" asked Emma. "You want to ask Josephine for her autograph?"

"Yeah, maybe," said Ant as she rummaged through her backpack. "Remember what Cecilia said? Whoever goes out to the old infirmary signs their name on one of the walls. So this is in case no one else thinks about bringing a pen." She held up a black Sharpie like a trophy, then dropped it into her pants pocket. "Okay, let's go."

We held on to each other as we fumbled through the dark on the way to cabin twenty, where the other girls were gathered.

A tall girl with black hair counted everyone, then whispered, "Okay, we're all here. Remember, stick together, and stay totally quiet. We'll turn our flashlights on when it's safe."

Cecilia, Vivienne, and a few other girls led the way. After a couple of minutes of shuffling down the trail in the dark, the girls at the front of the pack turned on their flashlights; then the rest of us did, too. On the way through the woods, I tried to distract myself by listening for birds. All I could hear were bugs. Then a high-pitched shriek pierced the air, right above our heads.

Everyone froze. Georgie squeezed my arm. "What was that?"

"It sounded like a girl screaming," whispered Emma. "Maybe it's Josephine!"

"Just an owl." I didn't want to be a know-it-all, but it was hard to hold back when it came to birds. Barred owls were on the list Audrey had given me, and they have a screamy call.

We walked until our trail ended; then Cecilia pointed left with her flashlight. "This way," she whispered. How did she know where to go? It all looked like a lot of overgrown brush to me. After a gradual slope, the ground changed from firm to spongy, and smelled like rotting leaves. Cecilia turned to us and held her flashlight up to show off her creepy grin. "We're heeeeeere."

We swept our flashlights over the infirmary, which looked like the skeleton of a cabin with half of its roof. Holes in the rotten wood swallowed up our flashlight beams.

"Wait," said Georgie. "Before we go in, we need to make sure nothing is in there."

"Like Josephine?" said Emma.

"Like raccoons, or . . . anything," said Georgie. "Animals could be using that as shelter."

"That's not a bad idea," said Cecilia.

Maybe we all agreed it was a good idea, but no one took a step toward the doorway.

Finally, Vivienne sighed and said, "Okay, I'll check it out."

"Thanks, Farmer Viv," said Cecilia. "Be careful."

Vivienne leaned into the infirmary and pointed her flashlight inside. After checking around, she waved us to the door. "Looks good," she said.

Nothing about the cabin looked good, but we joined hands and stepped through the open doorway.

"This is so cool!" someone behind me whispered. "I can't believe we're really here."

It was kind of cool, actually. I tried to picture the infirmary like it had been a hundred years ago, as a cabin with a real roof, solid walls, and a nurse taking care of sick or injured campers. One wall was full of signatures, the names of girls who'd ventured out there. *Theresa McDermott. Julia Hernandez. Blanche was here.*

One window faced the marsh. Beneath it, faded pictures of animals were etched into the wood. "This must be where Josephine's bed was," I said. A few girls gathered around me to see the drawings.

The full moon should have made the adventure scarier, but I was thankful for the light. On second thought, I wondered if it'd be better not to see what was out in the marsh, so close to us.

"Should we head back?" I whispered. Not that I believed in ghosts, but the cabin was home to more mosquitoes than people. The bug spray didn't seem to bother them. I smacked at my arms, then flicked off the squished mosquito bodies trapped in sweat.

"Yeah, let's sign the wall and get back to our cabins," said Cecilia. "But just think, this was Josephine's view while she was here."

The beam of my flashlight landed on something tall and white in the marsh. We all gasped, and my flashlight clattered to the floor. Georgie grabbed my arm.

Cecilia leapt back so far, she was at the doorway. "What was that?"

"No idea," another girl said.

I wanted to look again, but also did not want to look. Thankfully, my flashlight wasn't broken. When I aimed the beam out at the marsh again, the white figure still stood there. A sharp screech pierced the air.

"It's Josephine!" shouted Emma.

The other girls ran out of the cabin, but I was frozen in place.

The light landed on an eye. The eye itself wasn't surprising—lots of animals lived in the marsh—but this eye belonged to something tall. I couldn't tell in the dark how far away we were from each other, but I'd never seen a bird that size before. Not in the wild, anyway. Ostriches at the zoo were taller.

The moonlight shone on its feathers, white against the night marsh. When the bird spread its wings, it looked like they'd stretch from one side of the cabin to the other.

I'd swear it was a whooping crane, but I didn't think whooping cranes lived around here. Wouldn't Audrey have mentioned them when she told me about the other marsh birds? This was a lot bigger than a heron or an ibis.

I turned off my light. Whatever it was, I didn't want to bother it any more than we already had. The darkness made me feel even more alone in the rickety old infirmary. This was a lot worse than being left at Buc-ee's. I didn't have Wanda to chat with over ice cream cones and tell me that animals recognized good people.

From the doorway, I stared out at the dark woods. Well, we agreed we'd bail if things got too scary. Thinking you saw a marsh ghost was a good reason to take off.

Somehow, I'd have to get back to the cabin by myself. We'd taken a few turns in the trail on the way, but I hadn't paid attention since we were just following along. Having my phone would've been nice. Not that I would've called anyone, but the phone's map would have pointed me in the right direction.

Walking into the cabin after the others left me at the infirmary would be super awkward. But I couldn't go back to my room at Aunt Audrey's cabin, either. I'd have to explain why I was sleeping in my own room and not with the Oddballs.

As I stepped from the cabin onto the ground, I saw the beam of flashlights. The lights bounced closer; then a voice whispered, "Nina?"

"Yeah, I'm here." They had come back. Luckily, the darkness hid the tears that were pooling in the corners of my eyes.

After a group hug, Ant asked, "Are you okay? I'm so sorry. We're the worst."

"I'm okay."

"We ran up to the trail and realized you weren't with us," said Georgie.

We found our sort-of-beaten path and started back together. Some of the girls apologized for taking off and leaving me there.

"We got so scared because of that ghost . . . or whatever," said Cecilia. "I can't believe you were brave enough to stay there!"

"It was a bird," I said. "A really big white bird. Thanks for coming back for me."

"Of course we came back," said Ant. "Buddy system, right?"

Georgie put an arm around me and said, "That's right. We watch out for each other. No one gets left behind."

I felt a little less like a mismatched cuckoo egg then.

Chapter 9

By morning, I'd almost convinced myself the bird wasn't real. After telling the Oddballs I'd catch up with them later, I ran to Audrey's cabin. I had to figure out what I'd seen in the marsh.

My phone showed a missed call from Mom, so I called back to find out when she'd pick me up. She had a busy weekend planned but could come get me on Monday. Two more days.

I opened my favorite birding app to search for the marsh bird. It did kind of look like a heron. White feathers, long legs, pointy beak. But so much bigger. A sandhill crane was the right size, but its feathers were gray. Maybe the moonlight had made the bird in the marsh look white. That had to be it. I scanned the camp's bird list, then checked it again. Sandhill cranes didn't live there, either. Not in the summertime, anyway. Sometimes they showed up in the winter. Whooping cranes weren't on the list at all.

Below the sandhill crane info on the app was a row of pictures labeled *Similar birds*. The first one was a whooping crane. A red banner beneath the photo read *Highly endangered*. They were taller and whiter than sandhills, with patches of red on their heads. I closed my eyes and tried to picture the marsh bird but couldn't remember seeing any red. Maybe it had been too dark to tell. But whooping cranes didn't live in this area either, no matter the season. One flock lived in Louisiana, and some from Canada migrated to the Texas coast every winter.

The more I stared at the pictures, the more they looked like the bird in the marsh. An online search for whooping cranes in Bee Holler didn't bring up anything. One site had maps showing where they used to live. A long time ago, North America had thousands of whooping cranes. Then they nearly went extinct, because people hunted them so much and they lost a lot of their habitats. Now there were about eight hundred. Some used to live in this part of Texas, a hundred years ago.

Somehow, I had to see that bird again. That meant going back to the old infirmary, but I'd never find it on my own. I didn't want to tell the other girls why I wanted to go back, and they probably wouldn't be up for a return trip. We'd fulfilled the tradition, visiting the haunted infirmary at night.

But wait, we hadn't completely fulfilled the tradition. That gave me an idea. Breakfast ended in about fifteen minutes. Hopefully that would be enough time.

On my way out the door, I read to the end of the whooping crane page. *Because they're so rare and so much effort has gone into their conservation, each whooping crane is significant.*

I plopped down on the end of the bench at the breakfast table and said, "We should go back to the infirmary. Think we could find it together?"

The other girls looked at each other, then at me. "Go back?" said Ant. "Why would we do that?"

"Because we ran off before completing the tradition." I held up a marker.

"The signing wall!" said Georgie.

"That's right," said Emma. "We forgot the signing wall. Well, more like we were too busy running away from the ghost to remember."

"So what do you think?" I asked. "We should go back and sign our names, right? We were there."

"Let's do it," said Ant. "Should we go now, before activities start?"

"We'll have to make it quick," I said.

"Okay," said Georgie. "But these blueberry muffins are too good to abandon." She wrapped a napkin around her muffin as she stood up. "I'll take it to go."

After a few wrong turns and dead ends, we found the haunted infirmary again.

"It looks so different in the daytime," said Georgie.

"Yeah, not scary at all," said Emma.

"Well, not ghost-scary," said Ant. "More like 'it might collapse on you' scary."

We gathered around the splintery doorway and peeked inside at the bare wooden walls scattered with holes. I stepped inside first, testing the floor to make sure we wouldn't fall through. Obviously, it had held up fine the night before, but now that I had a better view, I didn't trust it. The floor was actually in better shape than the walls, even though it looked like it was made of a few different kinds of wood.

The other girls followed me in, and I went over to Josephine's window, hoping to see the bird again. Not much out there but dark water and marsh grass. I knelt down to get a better look at Josephine's drawings. Carved into the wall were pictures of a dragonfly and some small birds and frogs. The largest picture was a side view of a bird with a long beak. I ran a finger along the grooves of the picture. It sure looked like a crane.

The pictures weren't in color, but small lines marked areas next to the beak and on the head, as if those parts were darker. If Josephine had had paints or markers, I was sure the top of the head would be colored red.

I looked out the window again, at the same view Josephine had from her bed. "You saw it, too," I said.

Georgie joined me at the window and pointed to a mound of tan reeds. "Look, turtles!"

I hadn't noticed until she mentioned it, but a few turtles were sunning themselves on the reeds. Something about that looked familiar, but I couldn't figure out what.

Ant and Emma came up to the window, and we stepped aside to give them a better view. "So cute!" said Emma.

I peeked out at the marsh through one of the many holes in the wall. The whooping cranes had been here. That was a long time ago, around the time Josephine was at camp. She might have been looking at the last whooping cranes in Bee Holler.

"You first, Nina," said Ant. "It was your idea." She pointed to the signing wall—supposedly the reason we were there.

"Oh, right. Then we'd better head back before anyone wonders where we are."

"I'm glad you thought of this, though," said Emma. "It's interesting to see this place in the daytime, just on our own. Wish you didn't have to go home soon, Nina."

"Yeah, it's been fun hanging out with you," said Georgie.

"Actually, I don't have to leave." I took the marker from my pocket and signed my name on the wall. "I'm staying here."

Chapter 10

"So you really can stay?" Georgie asked on our way back to camp.

She looked happy that I wasn't going home. Ant and Emma had, too, when I'd told them at the infirmary. And that made me happy.

"Yeah, I can stick around."

Ant clapped me on the shoulder and said, "You just can't let go of us so easily, right?"

"That's it, I can't get enough of you nerds." I wasn't ready to tell anyone about the bird yet. I'd look so dumb if I announced I'd seen a super-rare bird and ended up being wrong. I'd tell them at some point, but not until I knew for sure.

"What activities are y'all doing this morning?" I asked.

"Is it nap time yet?" asked Ant. "Last night was fun, but I missed out on too much sleep."

"Art barn for me," said Emma.

"I'm going on the nature hike," said Georgie. "What about you?"

"Nature hike sounds good." Maybe the counselors would take us to the marsh. That bird had to be out there somewhere. "I'll meet you there," I told Georgie. I had just enough time to run to my room and send Mom a message, letting her know I'd like to stay at camp after all.

The nature hike started at the campfire area. I spotted Georgie right away, and recognized Cecilia and a few of the other girls. The counselors Libby and Fiona stood near the fire pit with two baskets on the ground next to them, one filled with small notebooks and the other with binoculars.

Libby and Fiona introduced themselves and welcomed us to the nature hike.

"Or as I like to call them," said Libby, "Florence hikes, after the author of this book." She held up an ancient-looking book with a faded red cover. "Who's heard of John James Audubon?"

A few girls raised their hands.

"Like the Audubon Society?" I asked. The website for Audubon Society came up whenever I looked up birds. It was a really old birding organization, and they had pictures of every bird in the world.

"Exactly like the Audubon Society," said Fiona. "Named for John James Audubon." More hands went up.

"Almost everyone has heard of the Audubon Society," said Libby, "but how many of you know about Florence Merriam?"

Some hands popped up, and Libby added, ". . . not counting if you've been here before and heard about her from me." All the raised hands lowered then.

"Hardly anyone knows who Florence Merriam is, even though she wrote the country's first birding guide." Libby held up the book again.

"That's the first one?" a girl in the front row said.

"This is it," said Libby. She held the book closer to the girl and said, "Can you read the title? I know it's faded."

The girl squinted at the cover and said, "*Birds Through an Opera-Glass?*"

Fiona held her cupped hands over her eyes. "Yeah, you know, the little jeweled binoculars you take with you to the opera?"

Libby laughed and said, "If you look up what the first birding guide was, you'll probably see other titles—"

"—written by men," added Fiona.

"—but Florence wrote her guide long before any of those. I think more people should know about her and the work she did. Back when she wrote this in the late 1800s, people studied birds by shooting them first, then examining their bodies. Florence pointed out that we can learn a lot more about birds by looking at them through an opera glass"—Libby held up the binoculars around her neck—"than we can by looking at them down the barrel of a gun."

Fiona picked up the basket of binoculars and handed it to me. "Your opera glasses, ma'am."

These binoculars were lighter than Audrey's pair. I peered through them at the trees around us. Pretty good magnification, even if they did feel like a toy.

Fiona gave me the basket of notebooks next. Each one had a small pencil stuck into the spiral. I passed the basket without taking one since I'd brought my own notebook.

"Here's what Florence said about going out to look for birds," said Libby. "I don't think she'd mind if we applied this to all wildlife." She held the open book close to me and tapped a yellow sticky note that pointed out what she wanted me to read aloud.

"'. . . go look for your friends. Carry a pocket notebook, and above all, take an opera or field glass with you,'" I read.

Libby closed the book and said, "So let's go look for our friends. This way, Florences!"

As we started down the trail, Fiona said, "Use your notebooks to sketch what you see. You can write some quick notes, too, but often you can get more information with a picture."

I preferred to stick to words. Finding out I'd be expected to draw something felt like showing up to a class to see *POP QUIZ* written on the board. I wondered what Florence would suggest doing if you weren't good at drawing.

Along the trail, we stopped now and then to watch the wildlife, like squirrels chasing each other around tree trunks and lizards blending into bark and leaves. Whenever I tried to think of a way to ask Libby about cranes, we stopped to observe something else.

At one point, we moved on after Fiona pointed out the different kinds of fungi growing on a fallen log. I stepped ahead of the group, closer to Libby. "Hey, have you ever seen whooping cranes?"

"I have," she said. "Not around here, of course. I saw them once in Rockport, where a lot of them spend the winter." Rockport had come up on some sites I'd looked at, showing the whooping cranes who wintered at the South Texas coast.

"They're majestic," Libby continued. "Hard to believe how tall they are—and the wingspan!" She stretched out her arms to show me. "We couldn't get very close, but just seeing them from the boat was amazing. Louisiana has a flock, too. They don't migrate, so they live there year-round."

"So there aren't any in Texas now?"

"No, they live in Canada most of the year, but they'll

be back in the winter. Ask your parents to take you to see them sometime." She held up her binoculars and said, "Take some opera glasses so you can get a good look at them."

Fiona raised a hand to stop us after we heard a bunch of birdcalls. She turned to the group and said, "Let's listen and watch. See if you can find who's singing."

We all stood under the trees together, listening to the jumble of birdsong. "The way to figure out what kind of bird sings what song," Fiona added, "is to focus on a song and look around to see what bird it's coming from."

"But so many are singing at once," a girl named Luisa said. "How do you pick out one?"

"Florence Merriam said that it sounds like a confusion of songs at first," said Libby. "But when you listen for a while, you'll hear the true songs."

When I tried to grab on to one song in the jumble, a chorus of high-pitched creaks stood out. I aimed my binoculars at the tree behind me. The birds perched on the branches looked like thin blackbirds. Some of their feathers shone dark blue or purplish-black when the sunlight hit them. One opened its beak and sang some squeaky notes.

"Who are they?" I asked. "The ones who sound like rusty gates?"

Everyone looked up at the tree. "Grackles!" said Fiona. "They do have a rusty-sounding song, don't they?"

We stayed there for a few minutes, pointing out different birds whenever someone picked up on a song. When we continued down the trail, Libby said, "See, sometimes you have to get quiet and stop listening to all the noise. Then what's really important will stand out. Good rule for life, too."

"Can we see the marsh?" I asked. "I'm really interested in marsh birds." True enough, even though I was talking about one particular marsh bird. And I wasn't *un*interested in the others.

Fiona checked her watch and said, "Okay, we have a little time." She turned down another trail and said, "To the marsh!"

"To the marsh!" we echoed.

"Florence would call that 'a good birdy place,'" said Libby.

Georgie bumped my shoulder and smiled at me, probably thinking of our excursion to the infirmary. When we got to the marsh, I didn't recognize where we were, and wondered how big it was. It didn't look like the area I'd seen from the infirmary, or where I'd been with Audrey. But the bird probably wandered all around the marsh, so this seemed as good a place as any to see it again. If we did spot a whooping crane, I wouldn't have to worry about how to explain to Audrey that I happened to find one near the old infirmary.

Fiona and Libby told us about the marsh wildlife.

I tried to figure out which direction the old infirmary was, but it all looked the same—water and plants and flying insects.

My heart leapt when someone pointed and said, "Look at that huge bird!"

"Oh yes, that's a heron!" said Libby. "That one's called a great blue heron, even though their feathers are mostly gray. Aren't they beautiful?"

We stood and watched the heron, walking on its stilt legs through the marsh. Its beak dipped into the dark water, then came back up clutching a frog.

"Ewww!" some of the girls said.

"Poor frog," said Georgie.

"That's nature," said Fiona. "Not always pretty, but everything has to eat."

I studied the shape of the heron. Could it be the bird I'd seen from the infirmary window? Even though most of the feathers weren't white, they were a light shade of gray. It was pretty big—over three feet tall, I guessed. Maybe the darkness and the moonlight and being scared about the ghost had twisted it into something bigger.

Maybe, but I didn't think so.

On the way back, Libby told me, "Oh, I did remember something about a whooping crane couple in East Texas."

"Really? Like, here in Bee Holler?"

"No, way north of here—Longview, I think? Two of

the Louisiana cranes wandered across the border and were living on someone's farmland. Something happened to the boy crane. I don't remember what. After he died, the girl crane just stayed there all by herself."

"That's so sad!" said Georgie.

"Yeah, it was," said Libby. "She's not there anymore. People who work with the Louisiana cranes picked her up to bring her home so she could rejoin the rest of the flock."

I started to say, "That's great that she's back home," but my voice caught in my throat. I gave Libby what I hoped was a normal smile, then stepped aside to look at a spiderweb that stretched between two trees. I wasn't interested in the spiderweb, but I didn't want anyone to see my face and ask what was wrong.

Now I knew what would happen if a whooping crane was here at camp. It would have to leave. Even though I'd seen the bird only one time, I liked the thought of it being here, so close. But a whooping crane needs to be with others. Those crane people would want to know. First, I had to find the bird again to be sure.

Chapter 11

After that return trip with the Oddballs, I could find the infirmary easily enough on my own. I didn't want to explain to anyone why I wanted to go back. If the bird turned out to be a heron or something like that, I'd feel dumb for making a big deal out of it. A beautiful bird, sure, but nothing unusual. Maybe there'd be a better chance of seeing it at night again, but no way was I going out to the infirmary at night by myself, ghost or no ghost.

If only I could sit and watch the wildlife outside the window all day. Kind of like Josephine did, but without the illness. Then I realized I did have a way to watch for the bird, even without being there. During free time that afternoon, I took my trail cam down from the tree and headed toward the marsh.

I kept glancing behind me as I hurried through the woods. I wasn't supposed to be out hiking without a buddy. What would I say if someone caught me? Maybe I could pretend I'd wandered too far while looking for a new place to set up my trail cam.

When I stepped off the trail to cross the leafy ground to the infirmary, I thought of my principal, Ms. Shelton, lecturing me last year about respecting boundaries. Well, this was a really important one to cross. If I was right about what I'd seen, one of the rarest birds in the country was living in the camp's marsh. And I wasn't bothering anyone, unless you counted Josephine's ghost, which I didn't.

Being inside the infirmary by myself was eerie, even in the daytime. The floor creaked with every step, which I hadn't noticed before. The view of the marsh looked the same as last time, with lots of grass and bugs and a few turtles sunning themselves on an island of reeds. No sign of the huge bird.

"Maybe you *were* a ghost," I said.

I crouched next to the wall of Josephine's drawings and ran my finger along the grooves of the whooping crane picture. That gave me an idea. I held a blank page of my notebook up to the crane and rubbed my pencil over the paper. The outline of a whooping crane stood out in white, against the gray I'd colored in. There. My notebook had a wildlife drawing, even though it wasn't my own.

The windowsill was really warped, but I found one part flat enough for my trail cam to sit on. I threaded the camera strap through a gap in the wood, then pulled it tight so a gust of wind wouldn't knock it down. It would take pictures and videos whenever it detected movement. If that bird was out there, I'd find out.

After dinner that night, I looked up the Texas cranes that Libby had told me about. That led to some posts by the Louisiana Department of Wildlife and Fisheries. The earlier ones were about the discovery of a whooping crane couple, Matthew and Linda, who were hanging out on someone's crawfish farm. Everyone was excited enough that they were in Texas, but then Matthew and Linda built a nest. Whooping cranes hadn't nested in the state for about a hundred years.

Later came some really sad posts. Matthew died after flying into some power lines, and Linda stayed alone on the farm. Since no other cranes were around, the Wildlife and Fisheries picked her up to drive her back home. I pictured a whooping crane sitting in the passenger seat of a pickup truck, riding down the highway, even though that probably wasn't how it happened. They would've put her in some kind of crate, in the back of a van, maybe. Another post said that Linda had paired with a boy crane named Todd. They'd had a nest the year before and hatched a baby girl called Alice. A family photo showed that Alice was almost the size of her parents now, and had just a few rust-colored feathers mixed in with the white.

I wanted to find out more about Josephine, too. Not the ghost story, but the real girl who'd been here at camp and carved those illustrations on the infirmary wall. Without a last name or the exact year she died, I didn't think I'd find anything. But after scrolling through search results from "Josephine," "camp," and "Bee Holler," a site with old obituaries came up. I stopped at one from a little over a hundred years ago, and I knew after a quick scan that I'd found her:

> Mr. and Mrs. Thomas Doyle are mourning the passing of their 12-year-old daughter, Josephine, who was attending a summer camp in Bee Holler, Texas, when she fell ill with tuberculosis. In addition to her parents, Josephine is survived by her sister, Beatrice, 10, and beloved dog, Scruffs.
> Her parents take some comfort in knowing that Josephine did not feel alone during her final days, despite being quarantined. In a letter home, she wrote that she was kept company by the wildlife she could see from her window.

Twelve years old. Just a year younger than I was. Josephine wasn't a ghost. She was a kid who came to summer camp to have fun and meet some new friends. Then she didn't get to do any of that, or anything else again.

Audrey came in while I was reading. I closed the site, even though she wouldn't be able to see it from the bedroom doorway.

"You up for one more thing before bed?" Audrey asked. "I'm heading to the art barn for a bit."

"What's in the art barn?"

"Art stuff."

"Right, but . . ." I thought she meant she had some work to do there, like fixing something or checking on supplies. "You mean you're going to just do art stuff?"

"Yeah, I like to go there at the end of the day sometimes. It won't take long."

"I don't know. I'm not any good at art."

"You think not being good at something ever stopped me? You've seen my paintings, right?" Those watercolor paintings in the office and cabin were Audrey's work. In some of them I could sort of tell what she'd been trying to paint, but others looked like swirls of colors bleeding into one another. Shards of her pottery were used as paperweights or bookends.

"Some of my favorite things are things I'm not good at," Audrey added.

"Well . . . I guess."

"Come on, let's go make terrible art together."

The art barn looked more like a cabin than a barn, with walls the color of the trees and a wooden ART BARN sign next to the door. Inside were several paint-splattered wooden tables, long enough for eight chairs each. The counter along one wall, also paint-splattered, had a built-in sink. Plastic bins of art supplies filled wooden shelves.

Audrey carried a bin labeled *Clay* to one of the tables, along with two vinyl place mats. With a piece of dental floss she pulled from a dispenser taped under the lid, Audrey sliced off a hunk of clay for each of us. She didn't give any instructions, just plunked the clay onto our place mats and started massaging hers. I watched to see what she was making. For a while she just rolled the clay on the mat; then she formed it into a ball between her hands before pounding it into a flat circle.

The piece of clay in front of me was so smooth, just waiting to be shaped into something. I made a fist and pressed it into the clay, then ran a finger over the hills and valleys my knuckles had created. Then I squished it all together and pressed it down flat, marking it with faint lines from my palm.

I wanted to bring up the whooping crane but wasn't sure how. If anyone had seen a crane in the area, Audrey would know. Maybe the lump of clay in front of me could become a bird, or something that sort of looked like a bird. I rolled it into a ball, then stretched one side of it into a tail shape.

Audrey laughed a little then. I covered my clay with my hands, worried she was laughing at my attempt at a bird. But when I glanced up, Audrey was looking down at her own clay. "I love working with this, but anything I make has to be air-dried. Sasha has banned me from using the kiln." She nodded toward the back corner, at a barrel-shaped thing that I guessed was the kiln. "Once I made a ceramic bowl that looked pretty good, I thought. Then, when it was being fired in the kiln, it blew up."

"Blew up?"

"Yeah, something about the clay being too damp. If there are little bubbles inside, they steam up when it gets too hot, and . . ." Audrey made exploding noises while her hands showed a clay bowl blowing into pieces. "Did some damage to the pieces next to it, too, which I felt bad about. Anyway, I asked Sasha if I could still paint the pieces of the bowl, and she said, 'Umm, I'm not sure what the point of that would be, but okay.'" Audrey laughed again. "She looked so sad, standing there hold-ing the wreckage."

"Those are the pieces in the office, and the cabin?"

Audrey nodded. "We saved the biggest pieces and threw away the crumbles. I enjoyed painting them, and they turned out kind of pretty. Sometimes when things go wrong, I'll say, 'Well, at least nothing exploded.' I couldn't say that this time, but there was something worth saving."

The room was strangely quiet after all the activity of the day. We were in this bubble, where the only sounds were the squishing of clay and the frogs and crickets outside the windows.

"I like to come here when I need to unwind, or when I'm trying to figure something out," Audrey said.

One side of my clay was looking sort of like a bird's head. I kept pressing down one side, then the other, so it wouldn't be so lopsided. "Are you trying to figure something out now?"

"No, this is an unwinding session. Some days are so busy, I have to remind myself to breathe. But if I'm trying to solve a problem, something about doing an art project helps me put it all together. It's like my brain needs me to get out of the way so it can think."

If only that'd work for me, that doing an art thing would show me what to do or say. Then I'd know how to tell Audrey about the marsh bird without getting anyone in trouble for the haunted infirmary trip.

"That's like what Libby said on our Florence hike today," I said. "Something about getting quiet and listening for a true song that stands out from all the noise."

"That's a good comparison." Audrey pounded a ball of dough into a flat circle again. "I think our brain works on the answer, brewing up a solution back there, but doesn't show it to us until we're occupied with something else. Maybe the brain is like a chef who's making a big mess in the kitchen—or an artist in a studio—and it doesn't want an audience watching the whole messy process."

I wasn't sure about any of that. I could spend all day squishing clay and still not know what to do.

Audrey glanced up and asked, "So what are you working on over there?"

"Oh, it's ... sort of a bird." The head was even enough, and I pinched a bit of clay into a tiny beak shape.

"Cute," said Audrey.

"Not sure what kind to make. Do you have a favorite bird?"

"Hmm, hard to pick a favorite. I remember watching the cardinals in our backyard when I was a kid. They'd sit on the feeder together, even give each other seeds. So cute."

"Libby said something interesting about whooping cranes today on our hike. A couple of them built a nest together in Texas. That hadn't happened for a long time. But then one died. The crane people took the other one back to Louisiana so she could have a nest and lay eggs with someone else. It was really sad, but it was interesting that they were in Texas."

"Oh right, I remember that," said Audrey. "Poor gal. Wonder how she's doing now."

"She has a new husband, and a baby. Well, a big baby. I looked it up earlier."

"Nice. Glad she has a new family after what she went through. A lot of them mate for life, did you know that?"

"Really?"

"Really. They'll keep building nests and having new chicks every year."

"I'd love to see one in real life. Libby says they're majestic. Ever hear of any living around here?"

"No," said Audrey. "I don't know if they've ever lived around Bee Holler. Maybe a long time ago, before it was Bee Holler. Good habitat for them here, with the marsh." She rolled her clay into a ball and returned it to the bin. "Okay, I'd better get to bed. Let's clean up and go back to the cabin."

"You're not actually making anything?" I asked.

"Not tonight. Sometimes I just need to punch some clay."

Chapter 12

The best time to go back for the camera's memory card was during breakfast. Some people woke up ridiculously early to go hiking before that, and activities started afterward.

It was cinnamon roll day, so obviously I wasn't going to skip out completely. After my second cinnamon roll, I told the other girls, "Gotta run. I'll catch up with you later."

"Where do you have to go?" asked Ant.

My first thought was to make something up. I could say I was helping in the office. But that meant lying to my new friends. I also wasn't ready to tell them the real plan—to check the trail cam and hopefully find a whooping crane picture.

"It's . . . something I have to check on. Maybe it's nothing. Okay if I tell you about it later?"

"Tell us about a maybe-nothing?" said Emma.

"Well, yeah."

"Okay," said Georgie. "See you at lunch?"

"Sure, I'll fill you in then."

At the infirmary, I sat next to the window and opened the camera to take out the memory card. I clutched it in my hand, wondering what images it held.

One of the articles I'd read the night before said people should stay at least a thousand feet from whooping cranes, to avoid disturbing them. I couldn't picture how far away a thousand feet was, but guessed I'd been a lot closer than that to the marsh bird. One good thing about the infirmary being so old and rickety was that the walls had plenty of holes and gaps. I'd stay away from the window from then on and watch for the bird without bothering it—if it even existed. There was still no sign of it.

Back in Audrey's cabin, I plugged the card into the computer to see what the camera had captured. A lot of reeds blowing in the wind and bugs flying past the lens. That was the problem with the trail cam—it took photos and video whenever anything moved. It didn't know what I was looking for. A setting for "interesting stuff only" would be nice.

Then one picture stopped me. Even on a grainy image

from the trail cam, it was obviously a tall white bird on a pile of reeds. Taller than any bird that supposedly lived in the Texas wilderness. Long beak, black feathers on the face, and a patch of red on the head.

I was right. A whooping crane was here at camp. I had to tell someone, but for a minute I wanted to hold on to the discovery of this impossible bird. Each whooping crane was significant, and no one else knew about this one. Maybe that was why I'd wanted to keep the news to myself for a while. Not so much because I hadn't been sure what this bird was until now, or because we'd get in trouble for going to the old infirmary. This might be the only time ever I'd know something no one else knew. Maybe this was how most people felt when they made important discoveries. I'd always pictured scientists rushing out of laboratories and shouting "Eureka!" ready to tell the world about a breakthrough. But before they announced anything, maybe they waited, hanging on to the moment that they were the only person in the world who knew it.

In another image, the crane spread its wings, showing black feathers at the tips. Then, in a video clip, something else came into view. A second whooping crane, wading through the marsh to join the first one.

I clapped my hands, hardly believing what was on the screen. Two whooping cranes, there in the marsh. On a still shot of the pair, I zoomed in for a better look at something on the second bird's legs. High on one leg were colored bands—light blue, dark green, and red. Attached to the other leg was a device that looked like a small black box.

Of course. A tracker. And the bands were like a bird ID card. I'd read about that but had forgotten until I saw it in front of me. Whooping cranes had leg tags and trackers so the people who monitored them knew who and where they were.

So I wasn't the only one who knew about them. That was good, wasn't it? I tried not to be disappointed. But it did seem weird that I hadn't found any news about these cranes. Maybe the people who monitored them wanted to keep it a secret, to protect them. They didn't want people scaring the cranes away by rushing in for pictures or to check whooping cranes off their birding list. That made sense. Bee Holler was a small town. It'd be easy for people to figure out where the cranes were if someone announced that they were here.

I studied a photo of the cranes standing side by side. One was a little shorter than the other. The shorter one didn't have anything attached to its legs. On a clearer picture, I zoomed in to make sure. Nothing. No tag or tracker. Maybe some cranes didn't get them.

A few photos later, the two cranes stood together next to the reed pile. Something about that looked familiar. I minimized the photos and went back to the articles I'd saved.

There it was—an article about cranes in a Louisiana marsh. Earlier, I'd only skimmed the article for whooping crane facts. I hadn't stopped to read the caption on the picture of turtles in the marsh: *Turtles resting on a whooping crane nest while the crane parents roam nearby.*

That was why those turtles on the mound of reeds looked familiar when Georgie pointed them out. Like something I should pay attention to. It wasn't just a pile of dead plants.

This was bigger than seeing a whooping crane. I'd found two whooping cranes, and they had a nest. I had to tell the Oddballs.

Chapter 13

In the Oddballs cabin after lunch, we sat on the floor to look over the photos. I'd brought my phone with me, even though it was supposed to stay in Audrey's cabin. This was an emergency.

"Here's what we saw that night. Whooping cranes." I held up my phone to show the girls a video.

"Whoa, they look so tall," said Emma.

"Five feet tall," I said.

"How did you get these?" asked Ant.

I kept my eyes on the floor. I couldn't hide my return trips to the infirmary any longer. "Well, I kept thinking about the huge bird in the marsh, and had to see it again. This is a big deal—"

They weren't going to let me breeze past that so

easily. "Wait, you went back out there by yourself?" asked Georgie. "Without a buddy?"

"Umm, yeah. Just a quick trip to set up the camera. Well, and then again to pick up the memory card. I didn't want to say anything about the whooping cranes until I was sure."

"Why is it a big deal?" asked Emma. "Besides that they're giant birds."

I filled them in on what I'd found out, that whooping cranes had come so close to going extinct and that they hadn't lived in this area for at least a hundred years.

"Around the time Josephine was in the infirmary," said Emma. "The alive human Josephine, not the ghost."

"Yeah. One of the drawings she carved into the wall looks like a whooping crane. She must have seen them from her window."

Georgie pointed to the photo of the mound of reeds. "Is that a nest?"

"I think so. Maybe they're getting ready to lay eggs."

Emma clapped her hands and said, "Ooh, crane babies! How exciting!"

"It is exciting," I said, "but we can't tell anyone about them yet. If word gets out, everyone will be running over here to look at them."

"Right, we don't want to scare them," said Georgie. "But we should tell someone, right? Like Aunt Audrey?"

"How do we explain how we found this?" asked Ant. "Without telling on ourselves for going out to the infirmary, I mean."

"Are there some, I don't know, whooping crane people to tell?" asked Emma. "That way we're reporting the cranes without getting ourselves in trouble."

"Like someone who doesn't care we were at the marsh?" I asked.

Georgie reached for my phone and said, "Yeah, someone who'll just care about the birds."

"The whooping crane people must already know about them, right?" I pointed to the box on the leg of the larger bird. "I'm pretty sure this is a tracker. Whoever put it there has to know where he is."

"Do the trackers show exactly where they are, though?" asked Ant. "And how far away do they work? Since cranes don't live around here—normally, I mean— these must be far from home."

I didn't know the answer to that. Maybe the tracking devices stopped working after a while.

Georgie pointed at the phone screen and said, "Here's a page about reporting whooping crane sightings. They even ask if they have leg bands or a tracker, so they must want a report anyway."

The online form asked for things like the location, leg band colors, and any hazards in the area, like power lines. I thought of Matthew again, and how Linda was alone on that farm after losing him. At least the cranes here had each other. I couldn't think of any hazards to the cranes. Just to myself, when Audrey found out I'd gone out to the infirmary on my own.

"There's a phone number, too," said Georgie. "The LDWF—Louisiana Department of Wildlife and Fisheries. They have a whooping crane program. Want to call them?"

I shook my head. What if I told them the cranes were here and they said, "Duh, we know"? They wouldn't say it that way, but that was what they'd mean. "I'd rather fill out the form." The whooping crane people would get a report, and I wouldn't have to talk to anyone.

"Do they check the forms every day?" asked Emma.

"The site doesn't say anything about that," said Georgie.

"They probably check it all the time, right?" said Ant.

"What if they don't?" said Georgie. "We should call in case they don't see the form right away. These cranes could be laying eggs soon!"

Georgie had a point, but I hated it. The whooping crane people might have a lot of messages to go through. Or maybe they didn't check the reports every day. These were the people who'd know what to do, and they needed to know about these cranes.

After a deep breath, I said, "Okay. Let's call in a whooping crane report."

Chapter 14

As much as I wanted to help the cranes, I hoped no one would answer the phone so I could leave a message without actually talking to anyone. But after three rings, a voice picked up and said, "Wildlife and Fisheries, this is Odetta." The phone was on speaker, and the other girls smiled when Odetta answered.

"Hi," I said. "My name's Nina, and my friends and I saw that this is the number to call about a whooping crane sighting?"

"This is the right place," said Odetta. "Hold on, I'll take down that info." It sounded like she was typing something, then she said, "Parish?"

"Sorry?"

"What parish are you in?"

"I don't know what that means," I said. At the same

time, Ant said, "Oh yeah, those are like counties in Loui-siana."

"I'm at a summer camp. In Bee Holler," I added, as if that would help. No one knew where Bee Holler was.

"Hold on." After more keyboard clicking, Odetta said, "Wait. You're in Texas?"

"Yes."

"Wow. And you're sure it's a whooping crane? Other big white birds live around there."

At first I felt defensive. I knew what I'd seen. But it made sense for Odetta to question that. "Yes. I can send pictures. They're from a trail cam," I added, in case Odetta thought I'd been out wading in the marsh to get close-ups of the birds, like a National Geographic pho-tographer.

Emma kicked out a leg and pointed to her thigh.

"Oh, right!" I said. "There are colored bands on one leg."

"Perfect," said Odetta. "That'll tell us for sure who you're looking at."

I scrolled through the photos to find one with the clearest view of the legs. "Okay, here it is."

After I told her the crane's leg band colors, Odetta re-peated them back to check that she had it right. "Okay, hold on." After a moment, she said, "Holy buckets, it's Willie Nelson."

"Willie Nelson?"

"We have a few whoopers named after country music singers. Reba McEntire is here, along with George Strait and Garth Brooks. We used to have a Dolly Parton, but . . ."

She trailed off before finishing the sentence.

"I figured you knew where he was because of the other thing on his leg. Isn't that a tracker?"

"It is. All of our cranes wear them, but the trackers don't last forever. That's why we're so happy when people send us updates, so we can keep up with them even when the trackers fail. Usually they stay close to home, but once in a while we'll have one that wanders off. We had one that flew all the way to Nebraska! Even though this flock is nonmigratory, they feel the urge to take off sometimes."

"Zugunruhe." I thought I'd whispered it, but Odetta heard me. She gave a surprised laugh and said, "Sounds like you've done your research! That's exactly right—our cranes don't migrate like others do, but it seems like they have that same instinct that tells them it's time to go. Anyway, Willie is kind of a loner, and he roams around on his own. Never that far, though. Guess he wanted to check out Texas."

"Oh, he's not alone now, though. Do you know his friend?"

"I'm sorry, his what?" said Odetta.

"The girl crane who's with him. Well, I think it's a girl crane. They look alike, but one is a little shorter."

Odetta was quiet for a long moment, then said, "I can't think of who that would be. What are her band colors?"

"That's the weird thing. She doesn't have any leg bands. No tracker, either. She's just . . . naked."

"That doesn't make sense." Odetta was mumbling, so I wasn't sure if she was talking to me or to herself. "All of our whooping cranes have tags and trackers," she said a little louder. "We put them on when they're just a few months old."

"Could they have fallen off?"

"No, those stay on there really well. And even if one thing came off somehow, they wouldn't lose both the tracker and the bands. You'll send me those pictures?"

"Sure, I'll send them now."

I attached the photos from my phone and sent them to the email address Odetta gave me.

"Okay, got them," she said. "That's a pair of whooping cranes, all right. There's Willie, and . . . whoever that is. We'll figure it out with a DNA sample, but that'll have to wait. We don't want to disturb them while they're nesting. This is a big deal. That hasn't happened around there in . . . I don't know, maybe ever."

"So that is a nest they're on?" I asked.

"We call that a 'platform' until eggs are in it, but yes, looks like they're nesting. They might build a few of those platforms in the area; then they'll pick the best place for their eggs. If you're seeing them there regularly, sounds like maybe they've chosen this one. And you said this is at a camp?"

"Yes, Camp Bee Holler."

"Is everyone staying away from them, or are they in the middle of things? They don't usually choose a nesting spot so close to people, but maybe they settled in before camp started and decided to stick it out."

"Oh, no one is near them. Hardly anyone knows about them." I didn't tell her they were in an area that was off-limits. Maybe Odetta wouldn't care about that, but it still seemed best not to mention it. "It's an old part of camp that isn't used anymore."

"That's great," said Odetta. "It's best if the cranes don't see humans, or even hear human voices."

A pang of guilt hit me. Hopefully we'd been quiet enough during our infirmary exploration. We were whispering most of the time we were there, and talking quietly when we went back and signed the wall.

"They, um, probably heard us when we first saw them. It was at night, and we were really surprised. We might have screamed a little."

"In our defense," offered Emma, "we were in a haunted cabin."

Instead of being mad that we scared the cranes with our shouting, Odetta laughed.

"That would do it," she said. "I'd probably think I'd seen a ghost too if I came across a whooping crane at night. Sounds like you didn't scare them off, since they're still hanging around."

"Right," I said. "We'll be quiet from now on—if it's okay to go out there at all." I'd stay away from the infirmary if Odetta told us to, but I really hoped she wouldn't say that. After seeing the cranes, I couldn't imagine not visiting them again.

"Is it possible to stay out of sight when you go? We don't want them getting used to humans, but we'd love for you to keep us posted on how they're doing."

"Yes, the trail cam is in the window of the old cabin. The haunted one. Not that we have proof it's haunted, but that's the story. Anyway," I continued, when Ant waved her hand in a circle as a "get on with it" signal, "we can stay out of sight inside the cabin when we're out there, and watch them through a hole in the wall."

"That'll work. This is a busy nesting season, and with you being so far away, it's harder for us to get there and check on the nest. We'll want to visit at some point, especially if there are eggs and it's getting close to hatch time. Who would I talk to there to arrange that?"

The four of us glanced at each other, as if someone would come up with the right thing to say. I didn't want to lie to Odetta, but also didn't want to tell her she was the only adult who knew about the cranes.

"My aunt Audrey is the camp director here," I said. Ant gave me a thumbs-up.

"Bet she's excited about the cranes," said Odetta. "Please keep us posted on how they're doing. If you see eggs in the nest, the hatchlings should make an appearance in about a month. Meanwhile, we'd love to figure out who that mystery whooper is."

Chapter 15

So many thoughts were jumbled in my head after talking to Odetta. She was a real whooping crane expert, and she was thankful I'd called. No one else knew about these cranes. The first whooping cranes here in a hundred years, and they were getting ready to lay eggs.

For now, I had a job to do. Odetta would need updates, with new photos and videos. I'd figure out when to visit the infirmary so no one would notice. If I got caught, Aunt Audrey would put an end to the crane visits. Plus, everyone would want to see them if word got out. Like Odetta said, it was best for the cranes not to see or hear people. And I wanted what was best for them.

"This is amazing!" said Emma, snapping me out of my plans. "A whooping crane nest, here at camp!"

"Hopefully they'll lay eggs soon so we'll be here when they hatch!" said Georgie.

"And I love a good mystery," added Emma. "Wonder who the girl crane is."

"Nina, can you show us how to work the trail cam?" asked Ant. "That way we can take turns checking it."

"Wait, really?" I hadn't expected the other girls to help with the crane watch. Doing it on my own would be okay, but sharing the work would make it easier. That meant fewer trips to the infirmary, and hiking with a buddy was a lot less noticeable than hiking alone. "You want to help monitor them?"

"Of course!" said Ant. "Like you said, this is a big deal."

"We should keep a notebook, right?" said Georgie. "Like to write down when we've checked the camera, and what we see when we're out there?"

"And promise us you won't go by yourself again," said Emma.

"Right," said Ant. "The buddy system, remember?"

"Okay, at least two Oddballs at a time," I said, before realizing I was counting myself as one of the Oddballs. No one objected, or even looked like I'd said anything weird. "How about for now we go out all together? I'll show you how to check the camera."

"If we hurry," said Georgie, "we can get back before free time is over."

Once we got into the infirmary, Emma said, "This really is different in the daytime. Hardly scary at all." She kept her voice quiet so the cranes wouldn't hear us, and I was happy she'd thought of that.

We each peeked through a hole in the wall to check out the marsh. One crane was standing on the nest—platform, I corrected myself. Hopefully they would choose this one for their eggs. If they'd built other platforms around the marsh like Odetta said, we couldn't see them from here.

"Remember what Odetta said," I whispered. "We don't want the cranes to see us." The girls joined me next to the window, where I showed them how to reach for the camera while hiding behind the wall. "You can open it without loosening the strap much." I ejected the memory card, then slipped it back in to show them how. "So you can leave the camera where it is and just swap the cards out. We'll check the photos and videos on the office computer or my phone."

"What about a notebook?" said Georgie.

I tore a few pages out of my birding notebook and wrote across the top *Date, Time, Observations*.

Emma looked it over and said, "How about our names, or initials, so we'll know who filled in the report?"

After drawing one last column labeled *Initials*, I put the pages in my pocket to take back to the cabin.

Once we were on the main trail, Georgie asked, "What

was that word you said to Odetta, about migrating? Zoo-something?"

"It's pronounced like zoo-gun-roo." I explained what I'd learned about zugunruhe, that the instinct to migrate is in the birds' brains somewhere, even for ones that don't migrate. "They get restless at migration time, like there's somewhere else they need to be." When we got back to the cabin, I brought up a map of North America and pointed to the Texas coast. "These migrating cranes hang out around Rockport in the winter." My finger traced a path from there to Northern Canada. "Here's where they live the rest of the year."

"Wow, they fly all that way," said Ant.

"Yeah, it's about . . ." I scrolled down to read more. ". . . two thousand four hundred miles. They stop and rest along the way, but that's a long trip."

"That's so cool!" said Emma. "But back to our little flock—the big question for now is, how are we going to tell Aunt Audrey?"

"We have time to figure that out," I said. "Odetta said they'll want to check on the eggs before they hatch, right? Even if they lay eggs soon, we'll have a month."

Odetta was right; Audrey would be excited about having the cranes here, nesting. Maybe she'd be so happy about it, she wouldn't care about our infirmary visits. We'd figure something out. Until then, she couldn't find out what we were doing. I remembered Cecilia slicing a finger across her throat when she talked about how tough Audrey could be. Maybe this wasn't as bad as setting off fireworks or keeping a squirrel in the cabin, but I'd rather not find out. If Audrey sent me home for breaking the rules, I wouldn't get to see the cranes anymore.

This was the most important thing I'd ever done. I couldn't let anything ruin it. Like that mockingbird at Buc-ee's, Odetta trusted me. She hadn't even asked if I'd be able to watch over the cranes. Even over the phone, she knew that I could do it.

Chapter 16

We settled into a crane-checking routine, with a pair of us visiting the infirmary each day during free time or after having breakfast. Before turning off the main trail, we'd check to make sure no one was around. If only there were activities on that side of camp, it would have been easy to explain why we were walking that direction. But then the cranes wouldn't have had as much privacy, either. We agreed that if we did get caught, we'd say we were out hiking and got turned around.

On each crane check, we swapped out the trail cam's memory card and peeked at the marsh through a hole in the wall. Once we got back to the cabin, we filled in the chart to record whatever we'd observed. The card reader stayed in my pocket all the time, ready for me to check the photos and videos when no one was around.

Sometimes there wasn't much to see. Windy days were the worst, with photo after photo of swaying marsh plants. I forwarded the best images to Odetta, along with any updates. We were seeing the crane couple at their platform more, but no eggs yet.

Odetta had emailed me the day after our phone call. She'd shown the pictures to the other staff, but no one knew who the girl crane could be. They knew where all their cranes were, now that we'd found Willie. Odetta thanked me again for getting in touch and for monitoring the cranes. *Remember to keep a distance from them,* she wrote, *for your safety and theirs. For now, enjoy watching them. It'll be interesting to see what happens.*

Could Odetta be mistaken about not missing any cranes? The Louisiana flock had over seventy birds. Not a huge number, but still a lot to keep track of.

One evening when we were watching crane videos, Emma asked, "Do you think the girl crane could be from that migrating flock? That would explain why she doesn't have leg bands, right?"

"Right," said Ant. "If all the Louisiana cranes are tagged, she must be from somewhere else. Or could she have hatched in the wild without anyone noticing?"

"Maybe," I said, "but it's hard to imagine no one noticing a five-foot-tall white bird. Odetta said if this was wintertime, it could be a lost crane from the coastal flock. But those cranes migrated back to Canada two months ago."

Emma said, "Maybe one of those cranes got lost last winter, then met up with Willie Nelson and decided to stay instead of migrating. Once I went to a haunted house with some friends, and when I walked out at the end I was somehow holding hands with a boy I didn't know."

"Sure, 'somehow,'" said Ant.

"It really was an accident!" said Emma. "We looked at each other, horrified, and then I ran off to find my friends. Anyway, maybe these two accidentally met up and kept hanging out together."

"What if she escaped from a zoo?" asked Georgie. "Like that flamingo—you know about him? He came from a zoo in Kansas, and he lives at a Texas beach now."

"Let's check," said Ant. "It'd be in the news if one escaped, right? Losing a whooping crane would be a lot bigger problem than losing a flamingo."

We searched online and found a few zoos with whooping cranes. No reports of any escapes. "Still, I'd love to find out who the girl crane is," I said. "It doesn't seem right, does it, that no one knows her?"

"No one except for Willie Nelson," said Ant, "but we can't ask him. I mean, we *could*, but we wouldn't understand the answer."

"I wonder how the cranes tell each other apart," I

said. "They look the same, and they're all pretty closely related." One of the online articles said that all the whooping cranes alive now descended from the fifteen or so that were left in the early 1940s, when they almost went extinct. I wished my birding apps could ID individual birds, instead of just the species.

"But that's like a lot of animals, right?" said Georgie. "Like all polar bears or alligators or whatever look the same to us, but they recognize each other. Or like on that penguin documentary, where the penguin moms and dads find each other by calling."

"Oh yeah, I saw that!" said Ant. "A whole mob of penguins calling at once, but they follow the right call."

"Maybe the cranes recognize each other's voices," I said.

"If only they had fingerprints," said Emma. "Or like, beak prints or something."

"Does it matter that we don't know who that crane is, though?" asked Ant. "Odetta said they'll figure it out later with DNA, right?"

"Right, but she also said it would give them some good information, like if she's been a mom before. Some cranes haven't been able to hatch their own eggs, but they've been good adoptive parents to other birds' chicks. Maybe she has experience being a parent and knows what she's doing, or—"

"—or she's just winging it?" said Ant.

We all groaned, then laughed. I tossed a pillow at Ant, but she caught it before it hit her in the face.

"Wouldn't it be fun if we solved the crane mystery?" said Emma. She pulled a book from the stack on the dresser. "We could be detectives, like Nessie McGee. Have you read any of the series?"

When we shook our heads, Emma continued, "Oh, you have to! Nessie's my favorite detective. She says when you're trying to solve a mystery, it's important to keep your eyes open for clues wherever you go. She notices things other people don't. But you have to watch out for red herrings, too."

"Herring?" said Ant. "Isn't that a fish?"

"No," said Emma. "Well, yeah, I guess it is a fish, but in a mystery, it means something that leads the detective down the wrong path. An answer that makes sense but ends up being a false clue. You know how if you're watching a movie and you think you know who the bad guy is? Well, if it's early in the story, it's probably a red herring. The real solution is still out there." Emma pulled another book from the middle of the stack. "Like in *Nessie McGee and the Lake Monster*, it seemed like mean taxidermist Jethro Muggins was the bad guy, but turned out it was geologist Jeff. I guess I've spoiled that story for you if you planned to read it, but there are thirty more books in the series."

"So how do you know something is a red herring, if it's a solution that makes sense?" asked Georgie.

"Well, you don't," said Emma. "That's what makes it hard. The detective only figures out the mystery after they discover a new clue or realize what they've over-looked all along."

None of this had anything to do with the cranes. I didn't need to figure out the bad guy in a mystery novel, I just needed to know who that crane was. Every whooping crane was significant. And these cranes were especially significant, because of where they were. Of all places, they showed up in Bee Holler, Texas. It wasn't right that no one knew her name.

Chapter 17

Rainy days were worse than windy days. Rain meant no going to the infirmary—all outdoor activities were canceled, so it'd be way too obvious if we went hiking in the pouring rain. Those days, I had to just wonder how the cranes were doing and what photos were sitting on the memory card. Hopefully more than just swaying plants and rain.

One morning, we were soaked after the short run from breakfast to the Oddballs cabin, with the wind blowing the rain sideways. After changing into dry clothes, I flopped onto a bed and pulled up the covers.

"Wonder what the cranes do when it's raining like this," I said.

"Hang out under some trees, maybe," said Emma.

"Guess we'll see whenever we can check the camera

again," said Ant. "Till then, we need something to distract us."

"Maybe a game?" I said, even though nothing would take my mind off the cranes.

"Another round of truth or truth?" said Emma.

"Okay," said Georgie. "Who's first?"

"I have one for Ant!" said Emma. "Truth—why are you called Ant? And don't tell us it's because you like ants. There's more to it than that."

Ant sighed and said, "Fine. But it doesn't leave this cabin."

"Right," said Georgie. "Oddballs promise."

"Okay, this was in fifth grade, and we were outside for PE, playing softball. I was in center field. I can catch anything. Not many fifth graders can hit that far, but if anyone had a pop fly or a line drive . . ."

"We get it, you're a star athlete," said Emma. "Anyway . . ."

"Anyway," Ant continued, "my ankle started stinging and itching. When I reached down to scratch, fire ants were crawling all over me."

"Oh no," said Georgie.

"Exactly. I started yelling and trying to brush them off my jeans, but there were too many. Pretty soon the other kids gathered around, and then Coach Vogel came running up. She got everyone to back away and told me, 'Hurry, take your pants off!' I was so desperate for the biting to stop, I almost did take them off. But then I remembered . . . hedgehogs."

"Um, hedgehogs?" I said.

"On my underwear," said Ant, looking grim. "My underwear had little hedgehogs all over them. Hedgehogs wearing Santa hats."

We all groaned and laughed a little, feeling Ant's embarrassment.

"Yeah," she continued. "Do I look like someone who'd have underwear with cute little animals on them? And even worse, it was waaay past Christmas. I didn't care when I grabbed them from the dresser that morning. 'Cause who's going to see them, right?"

"Only your whole class," said Emma.

"I wasn't about to let that happen," said Ant. "I'd rather die by ant bite."

"What'd you do?" Georgie asked.

"Broke away from Coach Vogel and ran into the school, with every fire ant in town biting my legs. I ran straight to the nurse's office, yelling 'Ants!' the whole way."

We were all laughing by then. "I wish I could've seen that," I said.

"Well, here's a reenactment for you." Ant stood up and ran around the cabin, flailing her arms, face contorted in pain, calling out "Ants! Ants!" between pretend sobs. I was dying to hear how the story ended, but we were all laughing too hard for her to continue.

Ant sat on the edge of her bed and waited for us to recover from her demonstration. Georgie wiped tears from her eyes and said, "Okay, what happened once you got to the nurse's office?"

"Ran straight into the restroom and didn't even bother closing the door. Once I got my pants off and threw them in the sink, I used wet paper towels to wipe off my legs. The nurse came in and helped me get rid of the rest of the ants. I was okay with that—nurses have seen a lot worse than Santa hedgehog underwear, right? Honestly, I was so desperate for the ants to stop biting, I didn't care about anything else."

"Wow," said Emma. "So then what?"

"The nurse gave me some lotion to help with the itching—and some sweatpants from the lost and found, since my jeans were wet from being in the sink—and called my mom to pick me up. Mom gave me some Benadryl, and I spent the rest of the day watching TV and napping on the couch. Oh, and I had lunch detention after I got back to school."

"Wait," said Georgie, "after all those ant bites, you were in trouble?"

"Yeah, for running away from Coach instead of doing what she said. Also, the nurse's office had an ant problem after that."

We started laughing all over again, applauding as Ant stood up and took a bow. Then Emma asked, "And everyone called you Ant after that? That's a much better story about how you got your name, instead of 'I just like ants.' I can't believe you like bugs at all! I would think you'd hate them."

"Nah, they're all right. Actually, that's what got me interested in bugs—I started reading all about them after that. Yeah, I hated getting bitten, but ants will be ants. They were defending their home and their queen. Anyway, the name Ant fits me better."

"Wait, what is your real name?" I asked.

"It's Aurora."

"Aurora?" Aurora sounded like the name of a fancy grandma, one who likes arranging flowers and wearing pink.

"What's wrong with 'Aurora'?" asked Ant.

"Nothing," I said. "Just . . . yeah, Ant is a good fit."

"Okay, your turn, Nina," said Ant.

"Oh, me? My parents named me after my grandma. Which is weird, because I'm not the oldest daughter. They were going to give the name to my sister, but when she was born, my parents said, 'Nope, she doesn't look like a Nina. We'll name her Sage.' How does that make sense? Don't new babies just look like . . . babies? So they saved the name."

"No, I don't mean how you got your name!" said Ant. "Different question—what have you gotten in trouble for at school? Or have you been perfect?"

126

Something that had happened in the cafeteria the year before came to mind first. But it wasn't funny, and I didn't like to talk about it. Luckily, I thought of something else, something that wouldn't make me look so annoying. Weird, maybe, but not annoying.

"My best story isn't from school, but from science day camp. Does that count? The camp was a week long, but I only went for two days."

Ant squinted like she was weighing the decision, then said, "I'll allow it."

As soon as I started, I wondered if the story was too sad. Just thinking about it made me sad, even though it had happened a long time ago. It was kind of funny, too, though. Maybe the girls would think so.

"Okay, it's about fossils. . . ."

I told the girls about the science museum day camp I went to when I was almost ten, soon after Chloe and Aiden were born. I'd been counting down the days until camp started, when I'd get to spend every morning at the museum, learning about animals.

"Fossils are really rare, did you know that? I mean, it's rare to leave one. Most things don't."

"Yeah, I think I've heard that," said Georgie.

Emma shook her head.

"I've never really thought about it," said Ant.

"I never did, either," I said. "It makes sense, though. The animal has to have bones to leave a fossil, or something else that doesn't decompose for a long time."

Tuesday had been fossil day at science camp. We'd had trays of packed sand, with plaster models of dinosaur bones buried inside. We pretended we were archaeologists, brushing away the sand to reveal the bones inch by inch. The kids who weren't patient enough for that reached in and pulled out the whole skeleton, shouting "A T. rex!" or whatever they'd found.

Our teacher told us facts about fossils as we worked. She mentioned that most living things don't leave fossils. "There are probably millions of animals we'll never know about."

I stopped digging and asked, "What? Why?"

"Oh, so many animals went extinct long before humans showed up. Most of them died without leaving a trace." She shrugged and added, "So there's no way to know anything about them. Isn't that fascinating?"

No one else in the room had looked horrified, or like they cared at all. A couple of kids had exclaimed "Wow!" or "Cool!" Everyone kept digging in their trays of sand. That made me feel even worse, that the other kids could have fun with the activity, when I couldn't think of anything except the animals that didn't leave fossils. I'd never get to learn about them. No one would.

I didn't notice that I'd started crying until the teacher knelt next to my table and asked me what was wrong. Then the other kids noticed, too. I cried harder then, because fossils were a silly thing to cry about and I was almost ten and too old to be crying.

My mom had to come pick me up. Dad was at work by then, so Mom brought Chloe and Aiden with her. On the ride home, Mom kept asking what was wrong, like I couldn't possibly be so upset about animals that had gone extinct a long time ago; there had to be something more to it. Were other kids teasing me? Or was I sad about not being the youngest one in the family anymore? "It's a big change," she said, "having two new babies around. Maybe this has something to do with that? I know you're not getting the attention you're used to."

I looked out the window and said, "Just let me be sad about fossils."

That night I dreamt that I disappeared and no one noticed. In the morning, I cried all over again when it was time to go back to science camp. My mom tried to convince me to go, telling me, "But they're not talking about fossils today. You'll learn about something else."

It didn't matter. I couldn't stop thinking about those animals who'd died without even a fossil to show that they'd ever existed. Plus, what if I learned something else upsetting? What else would be painful to learn?

Mom tried to transfer me to a different day camp at the museum, but everything was full by then. Sage and

Declan had their own activities, so I spent the rest of the week at home and helped Mom with Chloe and Aiden.

Something we'd said since then in my family, if we were sad about lots of things at once or about things we couldn't explain, was that we were "fossil sad."

After telling my story in the cabin, I looked at the girls' sympathetic faces and said, "Well, it was funnier in my head."

They laughed a little, and Emma said, "That's so sweet, though! You poor kid."

"Yeah, really," said Ant. "That is sad."

I felt bad for bringing down the mood of the cabin, after Ant's story.

We were quiet for a while, until Georgie announced, "I told everyone about possum nipples."

Silently, I thanked her for saving the day. Once we all stopped laughing, Ant said, "You did what?"

"They're really interesting!" Georgie tried to hold a serious expression, defending herself and the possums, but some giggling broke through. "If you don't want to hear about it, though . . ."

"No, we *have* to hear about it now," I said.

"Possums have thirteen nipples, did you know that?"

We shook our heads. "I had no idea," said Emma. "Do they have that many babies at a time?"

"Sometimes more," said Georgie. "As soon as they're born, the babies have to crawl to the pouch and latch on to a nipple, where they'll stay until they're old enough to leave the pouch. If the mom has a bigger litter than that, only the thirteen who are quickest to latch on will survive."

"That's pretty cool," said Ant.

"Not so great for the kids after number thirteen," I said, "but that's really interesting."

"Oh, but here's the best part," said Georgie. "They're in a bull's-eye shape."

"What, each nipple looks like a bull's-eye?" asked Ant.

"No, I mean the whole group of them. That's how they're arranged. Twelve in a circle and one in the middle. Anyway, I was telling everyone at school. What was I supposed to do, keep that information to myself? I'd explode! You ever have that happen, where you find out about something so interesting, you have to tell the world?"

"All the time," I said. "I don't notice until it's too late that I'm being annoying." I'd never said that out loud to anyone, but it felt okay to tell the Oddballs.

"Well, I had to go to the office for 'causing a disruption.'" Georgie shook her head. "Some people just aren't interested in science."

"That is a fun fact, though," I said. "A bull's-eye."

"What if we had that many nipples?" said Emma. "Can you imagine the bras?"

We laughed so hard we had tears coming out of our

eyes. As the waves of laughter died down, Ant stood up and pretended to put on a complicated thirteen-cup bra. I could hardly breathe.

"I'd be late to school every day!" said Emma.

"Sorry, Emma," said Ant. "Set your alarm twenty minutes early to make time for all the boob-wranglin'."

Okay, maybe rainy days weren't so bad.

Chapter 18

Emma and I were on our way to the infirmary one morning when Libby saw us. Thankfully, we hadn't turned off the trail yet, but we were close.

"Where are you headed?" Libby asked. "Kind of far from everything out here."

"Hiking!" said Emma, a little too loudly. Her voice grew higher with each sentence. "Just a hike. Little pre-breakfast hike. Get the blood pumping."

"We love the Florence hikes so much," I said, "we decided to do our own." Maybe she'd be flattered enough not to ask too many questions. I looked up at the trees and said, "Looks like a good birdy place, right? Guess we got a little turned around."

"More like a lot turned around," Libby said. "Might want to take an orienteering class so that won't happen again. It'll be fun, too. There's one starting after break-fast."

Emma gave me a look that let me know we were thinking the same thing—it probably wouldn't be fun, but we couldn't get out of it.

As we headed toward the dining lodge, Libby looked back, like she was trying to see why we'd been walking down a trail that didn't lead anywhere.

I hated missing out on seeing the cranes, but orienteering wasn't so bad after all. Britt and Mindy taught us how to read compasses and maps, and how to look for landmarks in the woods. We divided into teams, then followed our maps, where we found directions to the next station. At the last station, the winning team—which was ours!—found a box of arrow-shaped pendants with the Camp Bee Holler logo on them, hanging on black cords so we could wear them as necklaces. We also got coupons for a free treat at the trading post.

"That was fun," Emma said on our way back to the cabin.

"Yeah, it was." I had almost forgotten about the cranes. Almost.

But Emma was thinking about them. "When do you think we can get back to the infirmary?"

I shrugged. "Probably not until tomorrow morning."

We caught up with Ant and Georgie and told them what had happened.

"We should watch for Libby before we go out there again," said Emma. "She'll be keeping an eye on us."

"Good idea," said Georgie. "Anyway, we're on our way to the pool for water basketball. Come with us."

I couldn't imagine being in the pool with a bunch of screaming and splashing. Plus, I was terrible at sports. "I'll just hang out at Audrey's cabin for a while."

"And do what?" said Ant. "Lie around and be sad about missing the cranes?"

"No," I said, even though that was my exact plan.

"Let's go with them," said Emma. "Everyone's clumsy anyway, trying to play basketball in a pool."

"If you hate it," said Georgie, "we can do something else."

I sighed. "Actually, I'm on my period. Think I'm going to take an Advil and lie down."

Ant put a hand on her hip and said, "Hmm, that's interesting, since you were on it last week."

After a deep sigh, I said, "Fine, I'll go change." I tried to look annoyed, even though I felt like laughing along with them. While storming off, I pointed at Ant and said, "But this is a sign that I'm spending far too much time with you Oddballs. Far too much!"

Georgie called, "And you wouldn't want it any other way!"

I let myself laugh then. Georgie was right. Maybe I'd never be Cool Nina, but Oddball Nina was better.

*　*　*

The next morning, we made it to the marsh without anyone spotting us. Emma and I peeked through the holes in the wall at the platform, where one of the cranes sat. With no view of the legs, I couldn't tell which crane it was. The only way to know for sure was to wait for the other crane to come back, but we didn't want to hang out at the infirmary long enough for anyone to notice we were missing. We were just making a quick trip to check on the cranes and swap out the trail cam's memory card.

"Pretty sure that's our mystery crane," I whispered.

"Willie must be out getting breakfast," said Emma.

Hopefully he'd come back soon. I liked seeing both cranes every day, and I also wanted to see if the one on the nest really was the girl.

Emma replaced the memory card in the camera and said, "I guess we should head back."

"Yeah, we should."

Just before I gave up and stepped away, I spotted Willie Nelson walking through the marsh. I waved Emma back to the wall. She looked out again and said, "Hey, you were right."

When the cranes called to each other, I said, "I wish I knew what they were saying." I imagined having a bird translator app that would tell me what their calls meant.

"Maybe it's something like 'Your turn for breakfast. Good fish out there today.'"

The girl crane stood and moved to one side when Willie approached, and they both looked down at something in the middle of the platform. They raised their heads and called out, a duet of bugles. They looked down again, and the girl crane nudged something with her beak.

Emma gasped. "Is that . . . ?"

"Yeah, something's there!"

"Something roundish, right?"

Could it really be an egg? I was afraid to hope. I so wanted to run into the marsh for a closer look.

"Let's get back to the cabin," I said. "We need to see what the trail cam picked up."

"So what do you think?" I asked. We were sitting on the floor of the cabin, passing my phone around and zooming in on the images from the memory card.

"Hard to tell," said Ant. She swiped through some of the photos. At that distance from the infirmary, the photos weren't super clear. "But it does look like there's something new here."

Georgie leaned over to get a better look. "Something roundish."

I wanted to believe it. We could actually have a baby whooping crane soon.

"Wait till Odetta sees this!" said Emma.

"I'll send the pictures from the office. I want to see these on a bigger screen first."

Before leaving, I filled in the date on the crane log. On the line for observations, I wrote *EGG!*

On the office computer, I zoomed in on the best photos of the nest. After comparing them to pictures of whooping crane nests I found online, I was sure we had an egg. I emailed Odetta, then stared at the computer for about thirty seconds before picking up the phone. This news couldn't wait.

"Wildlife and Fisheries, this is Odetta."

"Hi, it's Nina. From Bee Holler?"

"Hey, Nina! How's our crane couple doing?"

"Check your email and you'll see!"

I bounced in my chair while Odetta read my message.

"Holy buckets," she said.

"That's an egg, right? We have a nest with an egg in it?"

"Yes, that's an egg. And now the countdown starts— our due date is about a month away."

After a celebratory spin in the office chair, I asked, "What should we do here? Anything to watch out for?"

"Just keep doing what you're doing. We're so happy you're watching over the cranes and giving us updates. If they've noticed you're there, they aren't bothered by you. It's especially important now to stay out of sight so nothing scares them away."

"Does that happen sometimes? They get scared away from the nest?"

"It's happened. That's why when we announce nesting activity, we just name a general area. Some of the birding apps let people tag a location. The good ones will block that info if the bird is endangered, especially during nesting season. Someone posted about a whooper nest online, and people swooped in to get a photo and check 'whooping crane' off their bird sightings list. I understand getting excited about the cranes, but people crowded too close to the nest and scared off the parents. We waited for them to come back, but they never did. Fortunately, we were able to save the eggs and give them to other cranes to raise. Still, we don't want anything like that happening again."

Even more reason not to tell anyone about the cranes at camp. If word got out, that could put them in danger.

Something occurred to me then about the new crane that'd be hatching soon. "What about its name? Does someone there name the baby cranes?"

"They don't all get names," said Odetta. "Officially, they get just a number, but some have nicknames, like Willie. Actually, since you discovered this nest, you could choose a name."

"Wait. Really? You don't have to like, I don't know, take a vote?" I wanted to grab this chance to name a whooping crane chick but couldn't believe it was that easy.

Odetta laughed. "No need for a vote. If it weren't for you, we wouldn't even know about the nest. It makes sense for you to pick a name, if you want to."

"Yes, I do want to."

"Maybe a favorite singer or actor or something like that," she suggested. "Or a Texas-themed name?"

"Okay. I'll think about it." I didn't really need to think about it, but I wasn't ready to tell Odetta my idea.

"Sure, no hurry. Watch for that egg to hatch in about a month."

After we hung up, I sat there for a minute thinking about what Odetta had said. I could name a whooping crane chick. The websites about them said that they could live for over twenty years.

One of the rarest birds in the country could have my name. For the next twenty or so years, whenever someone asked how this one got the name Nina, they'd find out about the girl who discovered it. It would be like leaving a fossil. People would know I was here.

Chapter 19

In the cabin that night, I updated the Oddballs on my call with Odetta, except for the part about naming a crane chick. I wasn't sure what they'd think about me naming it after myself. Emma made a countdown calendar, with *EGG WATCH* written in big blue letters across the top. After filling out the crane log, we crossed off a calendar day. Not that I'd forget how many days were left until hatching time, but it'd be fun to watch the big day draw closer and closer.

Georgie was lying on her bed with my phone, when she sat up and said, "I found something." She read silently while we waited for her to tell us more.

"Well?" said Ant.

Georgie looked up. "I don't know if it'll work, but maybe there's a way to figure out who the mother crane is."

She told us that the pictures of crane parents with their new chicks reminded her of our conversation about penguins recognizing each other's calls. "I wondered if whooping cranes do that, too. Then I found this." She held out the phone to show us.

"A whooping crane yearbook?" said Emma.

"Yeah," said Georgie. "Not every whooping crane is in it, but a lot of them are. There's a yearbook entry if they've interacted with people, like if they came from a captive breeding center."

"Or the Louisiana flock?" I asked.

"Right, all of those are here." Georgie scrolled down the columns on a chart. "It shows each crane's number, and a name, if they have one, their age, what flock they're part of, and other facts about them."

Ant pointed to one of the rows and said, "Look, there's Willie Nelson. Hey, do you think they sign their yearbooks at the end of the year, like, 'Have a great summer! It was fun sitting next to you in flight class'?"

"Yeah, probably," said Georgie. "The best part is they have recordings of the cranes' calls." She tapped an arrow under Willie's photo and the call of a whooping crane bugled through the phone's speaker while sound waves moved up and down on a graph.

"Whoa," I said. "So that's Willie."

"That is really cool," said Emma. "But how can it help us ID the girl crane?"

"Their voices are like fingerprints," said Georgie. "Even if they all sound the same to us, each one is different enough to identify. I'm not sure it'll work, but what if we got a recording of the crane? Is there a way to graph it like these?"

"There must be programs that do that," said Ant.

"So if our mother crane has ever been recorded . . . ," I began.

". . . we'll find her in the yearbook," finished Georgie. "We'll look through the graphs of the calls and see which one matches our mystery crane."

Could this really work? I reached for the phone, then scrolled through the pages. My stomach fluttered as I read the yearbook entries. This was even better than my birdsong apps. Instead of just showing me what kind of bird was singing, it would show me who the individual bird was. I could find out her name.

"We heard the cranes on that last trail-cam video," said Emma. "Could we use that, even though they're calling together?"

"I'm not sure," said Georgie. "I bet it's hard to separate their voices."

"Don't forget about background noise," said Ant. "All the crickets and frogs and wind. If only we could yell 'Quiet on the set!' and let the crane mom do a solo."

Odetta would be so happy and impressed if I could tell her who the crane was. But first we'd have to luck out with the trail-cam recording. The cranes would have to move enough to activate the camera, and call out at the same time. Maybe it wouldn't work, but it was as close as we'd get to a fingerprint. A voiceprint.

The last few yearbook pages showed cranes who weren't around anymore. The information included the date they'd died, along with the cause of death. *Predator attack. Drowned in floodwaters. Viral encephalitis.* Some had question marks next to the dates, with comments about why they were presumed dead, like if they were never seen again after a hurricane. I shook my head. I didn't want to think about the lost cranes and all the dangers out there. We played a few more of the calls. They sounded so similar, I couldn't believe they were different enough for individual IDs.

"This entry has a link," said Georgie. She brought up an article about a crane named Martha. Ant leaned over to read it and said, "Look, it's Odetta!" She pointed to a photo of a tall Black woman with short gray hair standing in a field. The caption read *Odetta Landry of the Louisiana Department of Wildlife and Fisheries examines the scene where remains of four illegally hunted whooping cranes were found.*

"Oh no, that's awful," said Emma. "Those poor cranes. And poor Odetta."

I couldn't stand to think of those cranes. Who would

do that to them? And I couldn't stand to see the pain on Odetta's face in the picture.

"Let's get back to the yearbook," I said. After Georgie returned to the yearbook site, I said, "If it's possible to find a voice match, I know someone who could help us do it."

There was someone who'd understand why I had to find out the crane mom's name. And she was good at working with technology and sound files, even though she couldn't hear them. I'd wanted to be friends with her so bad. But I got so excited that my mouth outran my brain. Or in this case, my hands outran my brain.

Iris was the coolest, smartest, bravest girl I knew. And I was so annoying, she'd changed schools to get away from me.

Chapter 20

Iris was the reason I'd started learning sign language. I checked a book out of the school library and watched online videos of sign language lessons. I thought maybe we could talk to each other and then become friends. But when I got to school and signed what I'd practiced, my signs turned into a jumbled mess. I tried again and again, telling myself to slow down and sign more clearly. But I kept thinking about what to say next, and other signs I'd learned, and everything got tangled together.

One day at lunch I tried to start a conversation with her. I'd start with something simple, then ask her to sit at my lunch table. The group of kids Iris sat with never signed much to her. A little finger spelling and note writing, but that was it.

As usual, she didn't understand me. I signed the

invitation again, as clearly as possible. Then again. When that didn't work, I tried to stop myself, but my body wouldn't back away like my brain was demanding. It was like there was a switch I needed to turn off but couldn't reach. I was too close to Iris, literally in her face. Other kids were telling me, "Nina, let it go. She's not getting it." I told myself the same thing: *Just stop.* It didn't do any good. Maybe with the next sign, something would make sense. But how could that happen, when Iris wasn't looking at me anymore? If I signed bigger, she'd look, she'd recognize something, she'd see that I knew something about her language, she'd see that I was still there. She'd see me.

I signed faster and with larger arm movements, trying to get her to understand just one message.

Finally, she pushed me away, and I lost my balance and fell. I didn't want to make a big deal of it, but I yelled when my elbow hit the floor. My parents were really mad. I told them I was fine, that it was okay. Not okay, really, but sort of an accident. Iris was trying to get me out of her space. I hadn't noticed how close I'd gotten while trying to talk to her.

After that, Ms. Shelton had a talk with me about Respecting Boundaries. Iris got in-school suspension for pushing me. She apologized when she got back to our class, probably because Ms. Shelton made her. I wanted to tell her it was all right. I signed that to her the best

I could, just that one sign. I hadn't practiced it, but I didn't know what else to say to her. I should've told her I was sorry, too. I wished we could've talked more. She had an interpreter with her; he would've signed what I wanted to say. But by then I was thinking Iris didn't want to have a conversation with me at all—not through her interpreter, and for sure not via my own hands.

Soon after that, Iris was absent from school for a few days. I worried about her and hoped she was okay. We found out later that she'd gone to Alaska with her grandmother to look for a whale we'd learned about in science class. They just took off, chasing a whale. What a wild idea, and so brave. When I heard she'd returned home, I practiced "Welcome back" so I could sign it to her when I saw her at school again. I wanted to say so much more. *What happened on your trip? How did you do that? You're amazing.* But I'd start with "Welcome back." She smiled a little when I signed it to her, so maybe I did okay.

Over the summer I learned more sign language. I was getting pretty good, at least enough to have a simple conversation. I practiced in front of a mirror, checking that my signs were clear. I'd start out the new school year just saying hello to Iris. That would be easy enough. I'd make myself keep my distance, and watch her face instead of my own hands. If she didn't want to talk to me, I'd stop. But maybe she would talk to me, after she saw how much I'd worked on my signing, and that I was Respecting Boundaries, stepping back to watch and listen. She wouldn't look away. She'd see me this time. We'd be seventh graders, and we'd laugh about things we did in sixth grade. We'd even laugh about the cafeteria incident. *Remember that time I tried so hard to talk to you that I signed right in your face? Yeah, I remember you crashing to the ground.* Then she'd pretend to shove me and I'd wobble like I was about to fall and we'd laugh all over again. We'd shake our heads and roll our eyes. *We were such twelve-year-olds.*

But when the new school year started, Iris wasn't there. Not in any classrooms, or the hallways, or the cafeteria. Someone told me she'd transferred to Bridgewood. That school wasn't even in our district, but Iris could go because they had a deaf education program. She was around people who really knew sign language, not just someone who tried to learn it and got so excited and jumbled that her signs didn't make sense. Instead of feeling sorry for myself, and angry that I'd ruined things, I tried to feel happy for Iris. She had Deaf people around her all the time now, instead of being the only one. She must have been so lonely, having no one to talk to.

Chapter 21

I didn't get into all that happened with Iris, only told the Oddballs about the girl who could help us ID the crane mom.

"And she's Deaf?" said Ant.

"Yeah, but she works with things like sound files and animal communication. It doesn't matter that she can't hear the recordings or whatever. She can see what the sounds are like from the graph, like the ones on the crane recordings."

When Iris was planning to track down that whale, she put together a song to play for him. I found out about all that later. She made some of the song with recordings from the band and orchestra students, and added other parts from apps that play the sounds of different musical instruments. Then she somehow put everything together. I didn't understand how it all worked. She could also fix anything. If something broke in a classroom, she was working on it before the teacher could even call a custodian about it. Maybe this was a totally different kind of thing, but if anyone could help us with the crane recordings, Iris could. First I'd have to get her to talk to me.

"I don't know if she'll be able to help us," I said, "but it's worth a try."

"We'll need a recording of the girl crane, though," said Georgie.

"Maybe we'll luck out and get one," said Ant. "Were there any on the videos today?"

I reached into my pocket for the card reader. Empty. I patted my other pockets, even though I always kept the card reader and spare memory card in the same one, on the front right side. "Oh no." I looked around to make sure it hadn't fallen out of my pocket.

"You don't have it?" said Georgie.

"When's the last time you remember seeing it?" said Emma.

When *did* I last have it? I thought back to the last pictures I'd seen. The egg. I'd been looking at the pictures of the egg in the nest and calling Odetta about them.

I stood up and said, "The office." I'd been so happy about the egg, and about Odetta saying I could name a baby crane, that I forgot to take the card reader out of the computer.

The other girls looked up at me, wide-eyed, probably thinking the same thing I was. Whoever sat at the desk after me would've seen the card reader, and probably checked out what was on it. Pictures of the nest might be right there on the screen.

"Want us to go with you?" Emma asked, but I was already running out the door.

As soon as I stepped into the office, I breathed a sigh of relief. The place was empty. I tiptoed to the desk as if I was sneaking up on it, then laughed at the sight of the blue card reader plugged in right where I'd left it. A shake of the mouse showed me the normal desktop. No whooping cranes or nest photos on display.

I flopped into the desk chair. Safe for now. But this was an unwelcome reminder—sometime soon, I'd have to tell Aunt Audrey about the nest. I had a month to figure out what to say. Then the news about the baby crane would overshadow everything else. Until then, I'd have to be more careful.

With the card reader safe in my pocket again, I ran back to the Oddballs cabin. They watched with worried expressions, then relaxed when I held up the card reader.

"Close call," said Ant.

"Yeah, I can't let that happen again. I'll message Iris now."

"Can't wait to find out what she says," said Emma.

"And hopefully we'll get a good recording of the mom soon," said Georgie.

I didn't mention that Iris might not answer me at all.

I'd messaged Iris once before, to ask how she was doing and how she liked her new school. She answered the next day, with something short like *It's great, thanks.* I didn't want to bother her, but I had so much more to say. *What's it like being around so many Deaf kids? What's your favorite class? Have you made a lot of friends? Did you change schools because of me? I'm sorry.*

Now I sat on my bed, staring at the phone and figuring out the right words to say. This first message would be short. If I explained everything about the whooping cranes now, Iris might see the long text and put off reading it. If she responded, I'd tell her about the crane voiceprints. We'd have to get a clear recording of the crane mom and figure out how to get rid of the background noise. No telling if we'd be able to do that anytime soon. But honestly, I wanted this chance to talk to Iris again. We could work on the crane ID together, and maybe even become friends. It'd be different this time. I would be different. Maybe she'd transfer schools again, so she'd be with me and all the other people we'd grown up with.

But I was getting ahead of myself.

I started the message with the best bird fact ever, the one I'd been saving for Iris. The one that was about whales, too.

Hi, Iris, how are you? I learned this interesting fact I thought you'd like. Did you know that if you slow down a nightingale song, it sounds just like a hump-back whale song?

I attached a link to a video I'd found that showed how the two animals' songs matched up when the speeds were adjusted. When the birdsong was slowed down and the whale song was sped up, their songs sounded the same. Graphs on the video showed that the whale and the nightingale sang the same song—as the speeds were adjusted, the lines on the graphs grew closer and closer, until they finally overlapped.

Anyway, I added, *I'm at a camp in Bee Holler for the summer. My aunt invited me since she runs the place. There's a whooping crane nest here, which is amazing since that hasn't happened here in about 100 years. (We have to keep that a secret so a bunch of people won't come here to take pictures of them.) No one knows who the mom crane is. It's a mystery, but we might be able to ID her by her voice. It's something you'd be good at. Let me know if you want to find out more.*

Sending that message felt like jumping out of the tree across from Iris's house.

At lunchtime the next day, I still hadn't heard back from Iris.

"She's probably busy," said Georgie. I wanted to believe her.

Finally, a text from Iris came up while I was reading in bed that evening. I sat up and held the phone to my chest, then peeked at it again to make sure the message was real. After a deep breath, I reminded myself to stop and think before replying. If Iris didn't want to help us, that would have to be okay. It wouldn't really be okay, but I'd have to pretend, then figure out a new plan.

That's so cool about the whale and nightingale song! she wrote. *I've never seen that before. Weird that they match up, like they're speaking the same language at different speeds. Anyway, I'm not sure I'll be able to help with the crane thing, but tell me more about it and I'll see if I have some ideas for you.*

I read the message again, hardly believing it. Iris had written back to me. Then I replied, *Great! Ok if I email you? I can send pictures and explain everything.*

Ok sure.

In the email, I told Iris about the crane couple and their nest, and added the link to Willie's yearbook page.

Here's a video clip of the cranes calling out together, I wrote. *Maybe you can see what their calls look like with some kind of sound app. To figure out who the mom is, we have to get a recording of her voice, without Willie making it a duet.*

I tried to get across how important this was, how unique whooping cranes were, that they never nested in Texas anymore, and that it didn't make sense that no one knew who this crane mom was. *I want to find out her name and tell the people who work with the whooping cranes. Maybe it isn't possible, but we want to try. She's too important to be unknown.*

That was enough for now. I didn't want to throw too much at her at once.

The next morning, I woke up to a new text message from Iris.

Ok, I'm in.

Chapter 22

Iris's message continued, *I stayed up so late reading about whooping crane calls. They're fascinating! I guess they really do make a sort of whoop sound when they call? I saw that the Wildlife & Fisheries staff posted the news about the Texas nest. You've probably seen it. People are really excited about it.*

Iris was ahead of me on crane information already, after just finding out about them. I hadn't seen the posts about the nest here. Either they hadn't announced it yet when I'd read the posts about Linda and Matthew, or I'd missed it. Odetta had said they wouldn't mention where the cranes were because people would rush in for photos and scare them off.

No, I haven't seen that. What did they say about where the cranes are?

Not much. People in the comments are wondering where they can see the birds, but the post just mentions the county.

Iris sent a link to the post, announcing the exciting news about the Texas nest built by Willie Nelson and his unknown mate. My brain was running ahead of me, with so many questions for Iris. I reeled in my thoughts so I wouldn't scare her away already. One thing at a time. *So do you think it'll work, getting an ID on the mom if we can record her?*

I think so. It'd be great to find out who she is. I did a test run using the recording of the two of them, to see what the graph of their calls looked like. I'll try to filter out the background noise. I don't want to get too technical and boring, but I could send you the graph and explain more if you want.

I had a better idea, and wondered if Iris would go for it.

Yes, I'd love to see what you found. Could we do a video call? You could meet the other Oddballs—those are my friends here who are helping me with the crane stuff. Texting is ok too, if you don't want to do a call. I'm so happy you're working on this!

I held back for a minute before sending the reply. If Iris said no, it would sting. But I wouldn't know the answer if I didn't ask. Before I could talk myself out of it, I sent the text, then closed my eyes and held the phone to my chest. When I peeked at the phone again, there was a new message.

Ok. Is there a computer you can use instead of a phone? Some programs have auto-captions that'll pick up most of what you say, and I can type in a chat window. I don't want you to feel like you have to use sign language.

I really did want to sign with her. That was why I'd watched so many online lessons. It'd be different this time. I'd be careful, and I'd learned more since the last time we'd talked. But I didn't want her to worry about that and change her mind.

Yes, there's a computer.

Is tonight at 8 ok? I'll send you a link for the call.

Perfect, I wrote. *See you then.*

I got ready for the day and ran to the Oddballs cabin before breakfast to tell them the news. They'd get to meet Iris, and we were a big step closer to figuring out the crane mystery.

The days at camp usually flew by, but on this day, the minutes dragged. In a few hours, I would see Iris again. Not in person, but close enough. Talking about the cranes during the video chat might lead to us becoming friends again. Or for the first time, actually. Iris probably never considered us friends. But we would be. I'd be a good friend.

I asked Audrey if we could use her laptop later for a video call with a friend from home, and she told me we could take it to my room. Hopefully we'd be able to talk about the cranes without her overhearing. I'd remind the other girls not to talk too loudly when they mentioned the cranes.

Emma and Ant brought the memory card back from the trail cam, and we checked it out in the cabin after lunch. I scrolled through and clicked on each video, hoping for a recording of the crane mom. The couple always called together, though. One crane stayed on the nest all the time. When the parent who'd been wandering around came back, they started their whooping duet before trading places.

After dinner I checked to see if Iris had emailed yet with a link to our call, and saw that she'd sent another text message. A long one.

Hey, I've been thinking about our call later. Wanted to message you to get some things out of the way before we're on there with your friends. Remember we'll have the chat window, so you can type whatever the auto-captions miss. It's great that you've learned some sign language. A lot of people give up and say "never mind" if I don't understand them, which is really annoying because then I'm left out of the conversation. But if you sign something and I tell you I don't understand, you need to believe me. I can show you some signs too, if you'll be ok with me telling you if you aren't being clear or whatever. Don't try to go too fast. Fast doesn't matter if the signs don't make sense.

My embarrassment came whooshing back. I'd been so excited to show off what I'd learned, and wanted her to see me as a friend, but I wasn't really looking at her. If I'd paid attention, I would've noticed how she felt. My signing probably looked like a bunch of noise to her. Libby said on our last Florence hike that we learn the most when we step back and listen. Maybe that wasn't only about birding.

Yes, I'd love to learn some signs from you, I answered. *Sorry I was so impatient before. I promise to slow down and work on being clear. And we'll type whenever we need to.*

A long minute passed before a reply came up. *Ok, sending the link to the meeting now.*

That evening we sat on the bed in my room for the call with Iris. I clicked on the link, then held Georgie's hand. She didn't ask why, just squeezed my hand like she understood I needed someone to hang on to.

After all the times I'd hoped to run into Iris, there

she was on the computer screen. She looked older. Not like an adult, but not so much like a kid. Did I look different to her, too? The same annoying Nina, or a more grown-up one? We used to see each other every day, and now a whole year had passed. Something else had changed, too. Iris looked happy. At school, she'd always looked lost and on edge, worried or angry or both. Her face seemed softer now, like the tension was gone. I was happy for her, and also sad at the same time. Happy that she was happy, and sad at the thought that some of that tension she'd carried was because of me.

Ant poked me on the shoulder and said, "Helloooooo…"

I shook away the memories and said, "Oh, right." I smiled at Iris and signed as carefully as possible, *Good to see you.*

That was an easy phrase, but my stomach tightened. I hoped I'd gotten it right. I waited for Iris to correct me. *It's okay if she does,* I reminded myself. I'd have to go on like it didn't bother me.

You too, Iris signed.

I exhaled, then introduced the girls, spelling out Emma's and Ant's names. They each smiled and waved at the screen. Georgie knew the sign language alphabet and wanted to introduce herself. That worked out great for me, since her name was longer.

Iris pointed to herself and spelled out her name, even though the girls knew who she was by then. She signed,

Nice to meet you, then typed the phrase in the chat. The other girls tried copying her to tell her the same thing, and Iris signed it again for us to follow along.

She switched to the chat window and typed, *Okay, on to the cranes.* She agreed that the challenge would be getting a recording of the crane mom herself. *Getting a clear recording at all might be hard,* Iris continued. *The people who uploaded the crane calls to the yearbook had pro equipment and programs to get rid of background noise.* She shared her screen with us and brought up a video, showing a black-and-white graph that looked like the ones from my bird apps. *Here's the recording you sent me,* Iris typed. When she played the video, the lines of the graph moved up and down with the voices of Willie and the mother crane. Iris paused the video and pointed to fainter lines and dots scattered around the graph. *The marsh is noisy, right? Wind and bugs and other stuff? To me it looks like static.*

When she played the video again, I heard the background noise more clearly, as if Iris pointing it out had magnified it. Wind, crickets, a chorus of frogs, and other bird songs.

I don't have the pro equipment, she continued, *but the sound editing programs I have are pretty good. I'll filter out what I can. To ID the mom, I have to separate the cranes' voices on the recording somehow. The one with the leg tag is the dad, right?*

"Yeah, that's Willie," I said. Text appeared at the bottom of the screen, matching what I'd said.

Looks like their calls are really different. Can you tell when you listen to them?

I hadn't noticed that. When the cranes called out together, it sounded like a bunch of overlapping bugles. I glanced at the other girls, who shrugged or shook their heads.

Watch, Iris signed. She played the video clip of the two cranes calling out as Willie approached the nest. When she paused the video, Willie's beak was wide open. *His calls are really long, and the mom's are short. Like he's saying whoooooooooop and the girl is saying whoop.* She hit play to continue the video, and pointed to Willie first. Holding her hand like a puppet, Iris opened it to mimic Willie's beak. When I focused on Willie, his long call stood out. She ran the video back a few seconds, then pointed out the mom's call. Iris's hand opened and closed in time with the mother crane's short whoops. Just like she'd told us.

"That's so cool!" said Georgie.

"It's like lipreading," said Emma.

"You mean beakreading," said Ant.

We groaned and laughed, and Iris held her open hands up to ask, "What?" The captions hadn't picked up the other girls' comments.

I started to answer, "Just a dumb joke." But then I

remembered what Iris said about people telling her "Never mind" when they didn't want to explain something to her.

In the chat window I typed, *Ant says you're a great beakreader.*

Iris shook her head and laughed, and I was happy we hadn't left her out.

"Now we can hear the difference," I said. "You really think there's a way to filter out Willie's calls?"

I'm not sure. If I figure out how to delete the whooooooops, that'll leave just the short whoops to work with. I'll see what I can do. Can you set up some other recording device near the marsh? Something that'll run continuously? You're missing whatever calls they make when the trail cam isn't activated.

"You mean like an old tape recorder?" I said. "I think I saw one in the office closet."

A cell phone would work, if you're okay leaving it out there. That'd be better, since it'd be easy to send me the sound file.

"Yeah, I think I could do that. Just leave it out there overnight, with a recording running?"

Or early in the morning, if they sleep during the night. Your phone should record for a few hours before the battery runs out. Long enough to catch if they ever call out individually. That'll be our best chance to find out who the mother crane is.

Chapter 23

Iris sent me a recording app to try. It recorded whenever it picked up any noise, and rested when it didn't. Kind of like the trail cam, but activated by sound instead of movement. With all the noises at the marsh, it might end up running constantly. No telling how long it would go before the phone died, but we had to try. The trail cam's time stamps showed that Willie and his wife traded places on the nest about every three hours, calling to each other as they did so. They were most active early in the morning, before sunrise.

The app also had a graph with lines that rose and fell along with the sounds it recorded, so we wouldn't have to listen to hours of marsh noise. We could fast-forward to strongest parts of the recording and listen for the cranes.

I stayed with the Oddballs that night since we'd have to get up ridiculously early. Georgie said she'd go with me to set up the phone. We wanted to start the recording before sunrise to catch the cranes' calls when they woke up.

A care package from home with fudge from Buc-ee's had arrived earlier that day, and I brought it to the cabin to share with the other girls. The card inside the box looked like one of the Buc-ee's billboards, with their beaver mascot announcing, *You'll Bea-Very Impressed by Our Fudge*. My parents each wrote a letter, saying they hoped I was having fun. A note from Sage read, *I think the birds in the backyard miss you. Is that weird?* I even got a note from Declan. A short one, about seeing a woodpecker in the yard. *I looked it up and found out it's a red-bellied woodpecker,* he wrote, *which is a dumb name because its belly didn't look red, but I figured you'd like it.* Maybe Declan missed me too.

I'd brought the stationery from my suitcase so I could write back to my family. After thanking my parents for the fudge, I told them that yes, I was having fun hanging out with the Oddballs and doing some birdwatching. I didn't mention that most of my birdwatching time was spent with two super rare birds. In Declan's note, I wrote that maybe the red-bellied woodpecker's name seems weird, but that their bellies are a little red. *They don't have a lot of red belly* feathers, I wrote, *but you'll see them if you get a closer look. Then the name will make sense.*

I told Sage that it was possible the birds missed me, especially the blue jays. *They're related to crows and ravens, who recognize human faces. They might remember the girl who usually feeds them. Peanuts are their favorite. Put those in the feeder and I bet they'll remember you, too.*

After lights-out, we stayed awake chatting in the dark for a while. Emma asked if I'd been friends with Iris for a long time.

"I don't know if we're actually friends. Maybe we will be one day." I told them a little about what had happened last year, without getting into that day in the cafeteria. Somehow I found it easier to talk about it with the lights out. "We were kind of friends when we were younger. Iris started going to my school in third grade, and our teacher assigned me to be her buddy and show her around. Back then that was all it took to become friends. You could just ask someone 'What's your favorite dinosaur?' and that was it. Then one day instead of answering the question, someone says, 'Come on, Nina, we're not five-year-olds.' How does that make sense? I know we're not five, but what does that have to do with anything? It's like there are rules everyone knows but me."

"It's like avoiding the shark-infested lava on the floor," said Emma.

"Shark-infested lava?" said Ant.

"Yeah, the hallways in our elementary school had red, white, and blue tiles. We'd pretend that the blue tiles were sharks and the red ones were lava. So we'd have to go down the hall stepping just on the white tiles."

"Well, yeah," said Ant. "Who wants to get burned by lava or eaten by a shark?"

"But halfway through fifth grade, no one was doing it anymore. Everyone just walked down the hall without even looking at what colors they were stepping on. Other kids rolled their eyes if I pointed out they were walking in shark-infested lava. Did I miss an announcement or something? I don't know how it happened, but it wasn't a thing anymore."

I was about to fall asleep when I heard Georgie say "Spinosaurus."

"What?" I asked.

"My favorite dinosaur. The Spinosaurus."

"T. rex," said Ant.

"Triceratops," I said.

"Pterodactyl," said Emma.

"Not technically a dinosaur," I said.

"I'll allow it," said Ant.

"Did y'all know that birds evolved from dinosaurs?" I said.

"Good night, Wikipedia," said Ant.

I thought I'd be too excited to sleep, but when the alarm went off I couldn't believe it was time to get up already. Georgie and I slipped out of the cabin as quietly as possible so we wouldn't wake Ant and Emma.

We kept our flashlights off until we passed the counselors' cabins, like we had on that first hike to the old infirmary. That seemed like so long ago. It was before I had these friends. Before I saw a whooping crane.

Once we made it to the infirmary, we kept our flashlights pointed at the floor, in case the beams of light bothered the cranes. The moonlight wasn't as bright as on our last nighttime visit, but I could make out the shape of a crane on the nest.

I set the phone in the infirmary window next to the trail cam. It was as close as we could get to the nest without wading into the marsh. Before starting the recording, I looked out at the marsh and whispered, "Let us hear your voice, just for a second."

After retrieving the phone during breakfast, we left it in the cabin to charge for the rest of the day. That night we sat together to listen to what it had picked up. The lines of the graph moved up and down, showing all the sounds of the marsh. I scrolled along the graph, stopping where the lines showed loud noises. Crane calls bellowed through the phone's speaker.

Ant clapped her hands and said, "Whoop, whoop! There they are!"

"Calling out together," I said. "Let's see if they do that every time, or if we got their individual voices at all."

It took longer than we'd thought to get through the whole recording. Sometimes the activity on the graph turned out to be a chorus of frogs, or other birdcalls. After listening to a few whoops while watching the screen, we got better at recognizing what the graph looked like when the cranes called out. We were almost at the end of the recording before we finally heard them calling out of sync. It sounded like Willie started the calls, which wasn't what we wanted. A long whoop went for a couple seconds before the other crane joined in. I forwarded the clip to Iris anyway, to double-check. *Pretty sure this is Willie, doing a short solo. Enough for an ID?*

"At least we know they do call out on their own sometimes, a little bit," said Emma. She could probably see the disappointment on my face.

"Yeah, we'll set it up again tomorrow morning," I said. "Maybe on the next recording we'll get to hear the mom. Hope I didn't miss anything on here." I ran my finger along the bottom of the screen to scan through the recording again, watching for any lines that indicated a crane call.

"Would be nice if the recording had a blinking arrow with *Whooping crane here* in big red letters," said Ant.

"Yeah, really." I stopped and looked up at Ant. "Wait. . . ." Maybe there was a better way to check the recordings.

"What is it?" asked Ant. "Don't tell me you do have arrows and big letters to show you the crane calls."

On one of my birding apps, I touched the list of birds beneath a recording and laughed. "Not quite. But close enough." I showed the girls the screen, which had a sound graph like the one we'd just been looking at. "This is a recording of some birds I listened to one day. But here's the best part." From the list under the graph, I clicked *Cardinal.* The graph skipped ahead and played the *chip-chip-chip* of a cardinal call. Then I restarted the recording and clicked *Blue jay,* and the squawk of a blue jay came through the phone's speaker.

"Wait a minute," said Georgie. "So this list . . ." She touched *Red-winged blackbird* and the *conk-a-ree* song played. "You've had this all along?"

I laughed and smacked my forehead. Ant flopped over, like going through the marsh recording had exhausted her.

"It's not a feature I've noticed before! I've used the app to ID birdsong and keep track of sightings, but I never thought of clicking on the list of birds to skip ahead to their songs."

Ant sat up and said, "Okay, now that we know what it does—this thing that's been in your pocket *the whole time*—it'll be easier to get through the next recordings."

"Will it record continuously, if you leave it running?" asked Georgie.

"As far as I know. When we go out in the morning, I'll let it run for a while before I leave it." If it worked as planned, tomorrow we'd be able to click *Whooping crane* from the list on the screen, and it would take us right to their calls.

Emma laughed and said, "I cannot believe you."

"Yeah, me neither." I'd have saved us a lot of time if I'd thought of this earlier, but it felt good to laugh about it.

Chapter 24

Iris answered my message while I was getting ready for bed that night. *Yes, that was Willie's call. Which is okay. It was a good test for the voiceprint matchup. Not a bad recording for a cell phone. I'm still not sure I can separate the cranes' calls. The voices sound so much alike, and they overlap. Hard to pick out what to cut. I'll keep trying, but it'll be a lot better to get the girl crane calling out by herself.*

Emma went with me to set up the next early-morning recording, then again later to retrieve the phone. When we checked it that afternoon, we saw that the app had four hours' worth of recordings. We got through it easily, now that we could skip to the crane parts. Beneath the sound graph was a long list of birds, some that I hadn't seen before. When I clicked *Whooping crane,* the recording jumped ahead to the calls from Willie and his wife. No solo calls. Hopefully Iris could find a way to separate the voices. The cranes calling out together all the time was kind of sweet, but I wished we could hear the mom by herself.

The next day, on another round of recordings, there it was: a quick series of *whoop whoops* rang out. Willie started his part of the duet soon after that, but we had it. A few seconds of the mother crane, calling out by herself. That call would tell us her name.

I tried to distract myself with camp stuff after sending Iris the recording, but it didn't do much good. We planned a video call again that evening so we could search through the crane yearbook together and find a match for the mother crane's call. I wouldn't be able to call Odetta with the news right away, since her office would be closed by then. And I couldn't leave that kind of news on a voice mail. I'd call first thing in the morning and tell her the mystery was solved.

We gathered in my room again with Audrey's laptop. In the office earlier, I'd printed the yearbook pages of all the living whooping cranes. We'd bring up the mother crane's call on the computer screen and compare it to the graphs on the printouts.

I took a deep breath and shook my hands out. I was about to jump out of my own skin, waiting to see the mother crane's voice matchup. Once we found it, no one else in the world would know the crane's name for about twelve hours. No one but the Oddballs and Iris.

"Okay, ready?" I passed some of the voiceprint pages to the other girls.

"Yeah, let's do it," said Ant.

We waved to Iris when she appeared on the screen. She smiled and waved back, looking as excited as I felt.

Ready? she signed.

"Yes," I signed and said aloud at the same time. "We're ready."

Listen to the recording first, she typed. *I got rid of anything that looked like background noise so it'd be clearer. Let me know how it sounds.* She attached the sound file to the chat so we could play it. No chirping crickets or croaking frogs, just a crane's voice ringing out from the laptop's speaker. Emma quickly hit the volume down button so Audrey wouldn't hear it.

I gave Iris a thumbs-up.

We held hands and watched as Iris uploaded the recording. A graph came up on the screen and Iris wrote, *Here's what her call looks like.*

The graph looked like a mountain range, with peaks and valleys showing the frequencies of the crane's call. Right in the middle of the graph, the highest peak stretched up to a sharp point.

"Okay, let's find her," I said.

Iris scrolled through the yearbook on her phone

while the rest of us scanned the printouts for a graph that matched the one on the computer screen. At first, I flipped through them quickly, waiting for that sharp mountain peak to jump out at me. Then I started over, checking more carefully.

"Find anything?" I asked the others.

"None in my stack," said Ant.

"Me neither," said Emma.

Georgie shook her head, then squeezed my hand.

We all looked at Iris on the computer screen. She shook her head, too.

"But . . . how?" said Emma.

"Yeah, what does this mean?" said Ant, even though we all knew what it meant. The mother crane wasn't in the yearbook.

Iris signed, *I'm sorry*, even though it wasn't her fault. She understood how much I wanted this.

I sat there, trying to think of what to say. It couldn't end like this. "Can we look again?" I asked.

Iris shrugged, then answered, *It won't do any good. It's the same recording, the same database. There's no match.*

I didn't want Iris to think I doubted her. She knew what she was doing. But I collected the pages from the other girls and rechecked the entries anyway.

Emma asked, "Do you see anything that's close?"

"I don't think it matters," I said.

Iris agreed, and added, *Not close enough. Her voice might be a little different with each recording, but it wouldn't be that far off. Remember, their voices are like fingerprints. She isn't here.*

"She has to be," I said. "It's like she's . . . some unknown whooping crane. Which is impossible."

"Obviously it isn't impossible," said Ant, "since she doesn't match anyone."

The hope I'd been clinging to slipped away. Odetta wasn't mistaken about not having a missing crane. Of course she wasn't. She knew her flock.

"She must be from some other group, right?" said Emma. "Like the ones that fly to Texas for the winter? Some of those cranes don't have recordings."

"No," I snapped. Emma let go of my hand and sat back a little. I took a breath. "Sorry. That's a good guess. But those birds are in Canada now."

She had to have come from somewhere, Iris typed. *Giant birds don't just materialize out of nowhere.*

This one had, though. "Cranes don't just lose their trackers and leg tags, either," I added. "This isn't making sense." How'd she get here? Where had she been until now? Why didn't anyone know who she was?

Maybe your crane people will have an explanation, Iris typed.

All the excitement in the room fizzled out. Instead of calling Odetta with the news about our discovery, I'd have to tell her we tried to figure it out and couldn't do it. I couldn't tell her the crane mom's name.

"How do you sign *thank you* again?" Ant whispered.

"Oh, right." I turned my attention back to the screen. Iris looked like she was waiting for me to say something else. There wasn't much to say, except to thank her. She'd had no reason to help us, but she seemed to understand why I wanted to figure this out.

I held my fingertips to my mouth, then moved my hand toward Iris. The other girls did the same, to thank her for helping us.

You're welcome, she signed, then typed in the chat, *Keep me posted.*

We waved goodbye, and Iris disappeared. Tears filled my eyes, and I tried to hold them back. Knowing that I shouldn't cry made it worse, just like at the museum day camp. The cranes were there, and their egg would hatch soon. It shouldn't have mattered that we didn't know the mom's name. Odetta and her team would find out in a few months. Still, I'd wanted it to be me. I'd wanted to tell Odetta who this mother crane was. Having the whooping cranes here was so special. Each one was significant. This couple was even more significant, because they'd landed in Texas. They'd chosen this camp for their nest. And since I was the one who'd found them, I was significant, too.

That was what I told myself. I'd discovered the cranes

and told Odetta about them. A new whooping crane would hatch soon. That was the important thing. It shouldn't bother me that no one knew who the mother was or where she'd come from.

That's how it is, being fossil sad. You can't quite explain everything that's wrong, and the sadness comes even though you know it doesn't make sense.

Chapter 25

Iris texted that night to see how I was doing. I was glad she did, since I didn't like the way we'd left things. It wasn't her fault that we didn't find a match for the mother crane's call. Even though we'd thanked her earlier, Ant shouldn't have had to remind me. I still wanted to talk to Iris about transferring back to our school, but this didn't feel like the right time to bring it up.

Doing ok, I answered. *Thanks again for all your help.*

Yeah, it was interesting. Just wish it had worked out better.

I did, too, but it had worked out, in a way: I'd reconnected with Iris.

It's a weird mystery, I wrote. *But it's been great working on it with you, and talking to you again.*

All of this reminds me of something a scientist on a cruise ship told me. She said that a fun thing about science is that we get to wonder about things that are impossible to find answers to.

That doesn't sound like much fun to me. I want to know everything.

I said the same thing! Iris wrote. *I asked her how whales figured out how to cooperate when they hunt for food together. I wanted the answer. But sometimes the answer isn't there, at least not yet. And Sura—that's the scientist I'm talking about—she's one of the smartest people I've ever met, and she's okay not knowing stuff sometimes. That way there's always more to discover.*

I guess that makes sense.

I had another idea. Iris might not be interested, but it was worth a try. If she said yes, it'd be way better than seeing her on the computer screen.

Hey, do you want to come here to camp? Aunt Audrey said I could invite a friend. You could see the cranes!

I waited for her answer. Maybe I shouldn't have asked. What if she didn't want to come? I'd feel even worse.

Thanks, she wrote. *It would be great to see the cranes, but I have stuff going on here, like robotics camp. You'll send me updates, right?*

I wondered if she really was that busy or if she just didn't want to see me in person. *Of course! And I understand you have other things to do. Just wanted to let you know you're welcome to come here if you want, like for a weekend or whatever.*

Wish I could. Can't wait to see the egg hatch!

Any day now.

Ant and I peeked through holes in the infirmary wall to watch the nest, where both crane parents stood.

"Not much time left," whispered Ant.

Our egg-watch calendar was filling up. One day soon, we'd visit the crane couple and see their new baby. I still hadn't told Audrey about them. I couldn't risk losing the infirmary visits, and seeing the crane couple with their new baby. But Odetta wanted to see them soon, too, and Audrey needed to know about that. I'd call Odetta later and find out when she planned to visit. I'd tell her that these cranes seemed like good parents. When she got to camp, I'd ask her if she thought so, too.

Telling Audrey about the cranes would also mean explaining how I'd discovered them. I'd try to do it without getting the other girls in trouble. Hopefully she'd understand why I had to keep the cranes a secret. Maybe Odetta could talk to her and let her know how helpful I'd been.

The mother crane waded into the marsh, poking her beak into the water. "It just bothers me that we don't know who she is," I said.

"That we don't know, or that you weren't the one to figure it out?" asked Ant.

True, the Wildlife and Fisheries staff would find out who the crane was in a few months. They'd replace Willie's tracker, put tags and trackers on the mom and baby, and get blood samples to take back to their lab. But honestly, I'd wanted to be the one to tell Odetta who this crane was.

I watched the crane mother and wondered, *Who are you?* She'd materialized out of nowhere and shown up in this place that had been craneless for a century.

When I got to the office, Audrey was storming out. The door slammed behind her. She stopped when she saw me, and glared. She'd never looked at me like that. I'd never seen her look at *anyone* like that. She looked angry and confused at the same time. There was something else, too, something I couldn't place.

"I just talked to Odetta."

Chapter 26

Audrey opened the office door and pointed for me to go in. This felt much worse than being sent to the principal's office. A whole flock of cranes flapped in my stomach. Audrey and I sat across from each other while she waited for an explanation.

"Whooping cranes?" said Audrey, like she could hardly believe the words. "Odetta said you've been visiting whooping cranes at the old infirmary."

"Well," I started, "I was wandering around one day, and ended up going off the trail, and—"

"Nina. The truth. I think you owe me that."

I'd known this day would come, and I should've come up with a better story. Or any story. "Okay. I went along with the other girls one night. They said there's this tradition—"

Audrey cut me off again. "I know, the first full moon. But I mean since then."

"Wait, you know about the infirmary?"

Audrey sighed. "Of course. I know everything that goes on here. At least, I thought I did. Going to the infirmary during the first full moon—that's been a tradition forever. News flash: a pack of giggling campers isn't great at sneaking around. But it's a big group that goes out together, so the counselors pretend not to know. They actually hide behind trees along the trail to the infirmary, to make sure everyone is safe. And Dale goes out there every year to replace any rotting floorboards and clear out the poison ivy." She stopped and shook her head. "I was happy the other girls invited you to go with them. You were making friends, and part of a group already. But I had no idea you went back after that. How many times have you gone?"

"Every day since then. I had to," I added, when it looked like Audrey was about to say something else. "I had to tell Odetta how the cranes were doing. But"— I wanted to get across how important this was without blaming Odetta for anything—"Odetta didn't know that the old infirmary was off-limits," I continued. "Or, um, that I hadn't told any adults here."

"You're right, she didn't know any of that," said Audrey. "She apologized for not checking with me earlier. She feels terrible. It didn't occur to her that she had to notify me, since she trusted that you had. I trusted you, too."

The words hit me like a punch to the chest. "I'm really sorry, Aunt Audrey." I couldn't come up with anything else to say. I'd been so happy to discover the cranes and watch over them for Odetta. But I'd made a big mess of everything.

Now I knew what that expression on Audrey's face was that I hadn't been able to place earlier. It was betrayal.

After that, we weren't allowed to go out to the infirmary anymore, not without Audrey. She agreed that monitoring the cranes was a good project.

But first, I owed Odetta a call, and an apology. I really, really did not want to make that call. The Oddballs offered to be with me. I thanked them but said I'd fill them in later. Apologizing to Odetta would be easier without an audience. I also apologized to the Oddballs, for dragging them into the whole thing. It wasn't hard for Audrey to figure out who'd been going to the infirmary with me.

"You don't have to apologize to us," said Ant.

"Yeah, remember?" said Georgie. "We wanted to go with you. And we love the cranes."

"Honestly," said Emma, "we'd have been mad if you'd

kept them a secret! We've had fun visiting them with you."

I was trying not to cry, but some tears escaped anyway. "I'm so glad I ran into you Oddballs," I said as they pulled me in for a group hug.

Once we let go of each other, Emma said, "And I know you said the crane mom couldn't be from that migrating flock . . ."

"Right, because—" I started.

She held up a hand. "But I've been thinking. We have to look at all the clues, right? The Louisiana cranes all have tags, and this crane doesn't. Plus, no one from that flock is missing, and her voice doesn't match anyone's."

I shrugged. None of it made sense.

"You know how Odetta said that their cranes don't usually migrate, but sometimes one of them does? Because of the zu-gun-whatever?"

"Zugunruhe," I said. "Yeah."

"Well, could it work the opposite way, too? Like a crane who *is* supposed to migrate just . . . doesn't? Or maybe started to, then took a detour? Maybe there's such a thing as a broken zugunruhe."

"A zu-gun-wrong," said Ant.

"Maybe," I said. "Or more like a broken compass. She started to migrate, like you said, but got lost or something." It was as good a guess as any.

"And then she found Willie!" said Georgie. "That wouldn't be a bad thing, right? The crane people will find out soon if that's where she came from, and she'll get her own yearbook page."

"That'd be interesting," said Ant. "Parents from two different flocks, having a baby together."

It would be interesting, even though I'd wanted a different solution to this mystery.

Outside, I found a tree stump to sit on and called Odetta. As soon as I heard her voice, all I could get out was "Miss Odetta . . ."

"Hey, Nina," she said. "You doing okay?"

It would've been easier if she'd been mad at me. Hearing her sound so kind made the words stick in my throat. After a deep breath, I said, "Yes. I'm just . . . I'm really sorry I didn't tell Audrey about the cranes. I didn't want to get in trouble for going to check on them, since we weren't supposed to be there. I was still trying to figure out how to tell her, when—"

"When I called and let the cat out of the bag," said Odetta. "Or let the birds out of the bag, in this case."

"No," I said. "Well, yes, that's what happened, but I don't mean it's your fault!"

"It's okay," said Odetta. "I know what you mean. Really, I figured the camp staff was in the loop, but I should've asked to talk to an adult there. I was so excited about you finding Willie, I didn't think about anything else. Could be that we both let the cranes cloud our judgment."

"Maybe that's it. I liked checking on the cranes for you, and didn't want to stop. But I still should've told Audrey about them. Anyway, I'm so happy you'll be here soon."

"Me too," said Odetta. "It'll be nice to finally meet you, and to see the crane family."

"Yes, I can't wait! We'll keep checking every day and let you know when the egg hatches."

"I appreciate it," she said. "Thanks for calling, Nina. I'll talk to you again soon."

"Odetta?" I said. "Do you think the cranes are good parents, from what you've seen on the video?"

"Yeah, they're good parents."

Chapter 27

The next time Audrey asked me to go to the art barn in the evening, I didn't make excuses about not being good at art. I'd been looking for small ways to make up for keeping the cranes a secret. I hated that I'd embarrassed Audrey, leaving her feeling like she got caught not doing her job well.

This time, Audrey took out watercolor palettes, brushes, and big sheets of paper, and handed me some empty cans to fill with water.

"What are you going to paint?" I asked once everything was in place.

"I'm not sure," Audrey answered. She brushed plain water over her paper with a wide brush, then added swirls of royal blue. "I'll paint some lines and colors and see what it looks like."

I did the same thing, playing around with how much water and paint to use. Where the paper was really watery, the paint collected in pools or spread out in blooms. Sometimes the colors blended nicely, and other times they turned into mud.

There was something I'd been wanting to ask Audrey, and it felt okay to bring it up then. Maybe talking was easier because we were busy painting.

"Aunt Audrey," I said, "you seem normal."

She laughed and said, "Okay. Thanks, I guess?"

"I mean . . ." Even after hanging around Audrey so much, I still hadn't figured out why my parents thought she was so weird. "An odd duck." "Audrey is Audrey." "Is that the influence we want . . . ?" I didn't want to hurt Audrey's feelings, but I wanted to know what the problem was. "What's the deal with you and my parents?" I glanced up from my paper to see if I needed to explain anything, but Audrey smiled like she understood.

"You know I worked at the family business, right?"

"Yeah, like a million years ago." I didn't remember Audrey working at the company, but my parents told me she had. They always looked annoyed when it came up.

"Yes," she said, "approximately a million years ago. Right out of college. I wore a suit and carried a briefcase into that shiny building every day. Can you imagine?"

I laughed. "No, I can't." Whenever my parents mentioned Audrey working there, I pictured her sitting behind a desk in her camp shirt, khaki shorts, and hiking boots. It didn't make sense—of course she wouldn't dress like that for an investment banking job, and she didn't work at the camp until later—but I couldn't imagine her any other way.

"That was the plan my whole life. I'd start working at the company after college and stay there forever. It never occurred to me to do anything else."

"Even though you liked being outdoors?" My mom told me that when they were kids and someone was looking for Audrey, their parents would say, "Look up. You'll find her in a tree somewhere. If that doesn't work, look down and you'll find her following some bugs."

"Yeah. I never pictured that being part of a job I could do. Outdoor stuff was for kids, or free time. I'd grow out of all that—that's what everyone said, and I went along with it. I'd get outdoors on the weekend. But no matter how hard I worked, I could never catch up. I was suffocating. The walls of the office were closing in on me. One day I took my lunch outside, just to enjoy the nice weather for a bit. When I heard birds singing, it was almost . . . jarring. I tried to remember the last time I'd heard a bird sing. Every morning I left for work before the sun came up and got home after dark. I looked around at the trees and couldn't remember what their bark felt like. This fear crept in, that everything I cared about was leaving me. I walked up to a tree and ran my hands along the bark. It felt like I was revisiting someone I'd abandoned. I stood there and said, 'I'm sorry.' I'm still not sure who I was apologizing to—the birds and the trees for forgetting about them, or everyone I was about to hurt. The plan wasn't fully formed in my head yet, but I knew I was about to do something I couldn't take back.

"I walked away from my job then—literally. Just went in for my purse and walked right back out, without talking to anyone. I'll never make that kind of money again, but look"—she waved an arm toward the windows—"I get to be here, all the time. Yes, it's hot, and buggy. I couldn't survive without the AC. But I can walk through the woods or kayak around the lake whenever I want. It's the best office ever. And I get to share it with a bunch of amazing campers every summer. There's nowhere else I'd rather be, and nothing else I'd rather be doing. I wake up every morning and can't believe this is my job."

"Wow." I set aside the paper in front of me, filled with watercolors, and started on a new piece. "So what happened after all that? After you walked away?"

"The family tried convincing me to come back, of course. Told me I was wasting my talent, and all that money spent on college. Some of them still do remind me of that. 'When are you going to stop playing around and get back to the real world?' 'When are you going to grow up and stop throwing your life away?' But what am I throwing away? And why isn't this considered the real world? What's more real than this?"

"Well," I said, "nothing blew up, right?"

Audrey chuckled and said, "You didn't see your grandfather. I don't regret leaving, but I do regret the way I handled it. I made a mess of things, and others had to pick up the pieces. I've apologized to the family for that. I didn't want to hurt anyone, and I was afraid of what would happen, so I didn't speak up. But it's hard to tell anyone else what's wrong if you can't even admit it to yourself. They still would've been mad, and disappointed—they'll always be disappointed, I think— but I wouldn't have caused so much trouble."

"I'm so glad you're here at camp," I said. "And that I got to come here."

"Me too," said Audrey. "Some people will never understand it, but I'm okay now with not fitting in. If I don't fit in somewhere, it means that isn't the place for me."

Audrey had never seemed bothered by what anyone else thought, but right then I saw that it did bother her, a little. She wished our family would see it, too, that this was where she belonged.

"Do you know about zugunruhe?" I asked.

"Zoo what?"

"Zugunruhe. Sage told me about it. It's what pulls

birds to migrate." I told Audrey about how the birds' brains tell them to take off, and they do, even if they don't know where they'll end up. "Maybe humans have something like that," I continued, "in whatever part of our brain we share with birds."

"Zugunruhe," said Audrey, like she was trying out the word. "Fascinating. Maybe we do have that in our brains, way back there somewhere. Far enough back that most of us don't notice it. And once in a while, it's too strong to ignore."

"So if someone gives you a hard time about walking away . . . ," I said.

". . . I can blame it on the zugunruhe," finished Audrey.

"I was going to say 'blame it on your bird brain,' but that works, too."

She leaned over then to check out my paintings. "So, what do you have there?"

I looked at the jumbles of color on the two full pages I'd painted. "Just, uh, paint, I think." Painting with the watercolors was fun, but my pictures didn't have any recognizable shapes.

Audrey pulled the first paper closer to her, then pointed out one corner where I'd brushed some flicks of red. The lines reached out in a kind of fan shape. Audrey turned the paper so the fanned-out part pointed down.

"Looks like a bird's tail to me," she said.

"Yeah, it does, kind of." I imagined adding some

rounded lines to make a body and a head above the brushstrokes shaped like tail feathers. Some of the feathers had clean lines, while some bled into neighboring feathers. "A watery bird's tail," I added.

"Hey, if we wanted realistic, we could take a picture," said Audrey. "This is art."

I wished someone had put it that way at my art day camp a couple years earlier. When I held up my painting of a tree, one boy said, "You're a real Picasso, Nina. But not, like, in a good way." Then the teacher lectured us about the genius of Picasso and his different styles, and said, "When you know the rules of art, then you can break them."

I hadn't been trying to break any rules. I just wanted to paint a tree.

"What did you make?" I asked Audrey. Her pages were swirled with even more colors than mine.

She turned a page to get a view from different sides, then said, "I'm not sure yet. Sometimes it takes me some time to figure out what I've created."

Chapter 28

We'd reached the end of our egg countdown calendar. Past the end, actually. We had to add extra squares after drawing X's over all the others. Maybe some eggs needed a little more time. That had to be it.

Whenever we got to the infirmary, I hurried to the wall to peek out at the marsh, expecting to see a little crane in the nest. Each time, the view was the same. One crane parent at the nest, and the unhatched egg in the middle.

Today, Odetta would get to see them, too. She was visiting camp later, with some other crane staff. In the Oddballs cabin, the girls stood around me as I squeezed another X in the margin of the egg calendar.

"It has to be today, right?" said Georgie. "Kind of a late bloomer, but the egg should hatch today."

"Yeah, I hope we get to see it hatch!" said Emma.

"Maybe it'll happen when Odetta is here," said Ant.

"She'd love that," I said. "That'd be kind of cute, wouldn't it? Almost like it's waiting for her, popping up and saying 'Here I am!' when she's watching." I couldn't believe I'd finally get to meet Odetta. The flock of cranes stirred in my stomach again. Even though she hadn't sounded mad at me, I felt guilty about not being honest with her. I wanted her to like me, and to think that I'd done a good job watching over the cranes.

Audrey had told the camp staff she'd be busy with a visitor for a while. She didn't tell them why. We wanted as few people as possible to know about the crane family.

I paced around the small office, stopping now and then to peer out the window. This felt like the first day at a new school and my birthday at the same time. Finally, I heard an engine approaching. A white van, dusted with red dirt, drove up the road to the office. Audrey held open the office door so I could be the first one out.

After the van parked, Odetta stepped out of the driver's seat.

"Miss Odetta?" I said, even though I recognized her from the poaching article.

She smiled and said, "That's me." She grabbed a canvas duffel bag from the back seat while two other people got out of the van. They each put on a backpack and took a broom from the back of the van. "And I bet you're Nina," said Odetta.

"Yes, and this is my aunt Audrey." My face warmed at the reminder of their phone call. "And these are my friends," I added. "Ant, Emma, and Georgie. They helped monitor the cranes."

"Well, we really appreciate it," said Odetta. "We're always happy to get updates about our cranes, and this one was extra special—finding out where Willie's been, and that he has a family." She introduced the two staff members with her, Felicity and Travis. "Felicity has worked with our whooping crane program for a few years, and Travis is one of our interns."

Ant pointed at their brooms and asked, "Gonna sweep the marsh while we're out there?"

"These are to keep the parents out of the way while we check the nest," said Felicity.

"Nina, want to lead the way?" asked Audrey.

"I'm ready to meet this little family!" said Odetta.

"It'll be nice to see Willie Nelson again," said Travis as we started down the trail. "No one knew where he was for months, until you called us, Nina. We were worried about him."

"Yes, we're so happy you found him," said Felicity.

"Me too," I said.

Once we got to the infirmary, the staff put down their bags and looked out at the marsh. I showed them how we peeked through the holes in the walls to watch the cranes while staying out of sight.

"Perfect," whispered Odetta. "An accidental bird blind."

The whooping cranes weren't on the nest, but they were wandering close by in the marsh.

"Good to see you, Willie," said Travis.

"And our mystery girl!" said Felicity. "Can't wait to find out who she is."

"Let's go check out their kid," said Odetta. The three of them took tall rubber boots out of their bags. As they pulled on their hip waders, Odetta said, "Now, it might look disturbing when we're out there. The parents won't like us intruding, but we'll make it quick. Just remember to stay quiet back here so we don't annoy the cranes any more than we have to."

Felicity and Travis grabbed their brooms, Odetta picked up her duffel bag, and the team headed to the marsh. Odetta crouched down and set her bag at the edge of the nest. Felicity and Travis waded a little farther, holding their brooms in front of them to keep the cranes away.

The cranes stepped toward the nest, calling out distressed bugles I hadn't heard before. "It's okay," I thought. "They're here to help you." I wished I had a way to tell the cranes so they'd understand. But like Odetta said, it would be over soon. Just a quick egg check.

Odetta reached over and placed a hand on the egg. She picked it up and looked over it on all sides, then set it down again and pulled something out of the duffel bag.

"What is that?" whispered Emma.

"Looks like a big thermos," said Ant.

I shrugged and looked up at Audrey, hoping she had an answer. She pointed out to the marsh, where Odetta was removing the top of the canister.

"Maybe there's water in it," said Audrey, "and she's checking to see if the egg floats."

"But why?" I said.

"Oh yeah, we did that in my science class," said Georgie. "It's a way to check if an egg might still hatch, or . . . not."

Why would Odetta need to check that? Of course it would hatch. It just needed more time. Georgie and Emma talked a little more about what it meant if an egg floated and what it meant if it sank, but I didn't want to listen anymore. I just wanted Odetta to put the egg back in the nest where it belonged.

She didn't put it back. Odetta pulled something else out of the duffel bag, a small red cooler with a white lid, the size that'd hold a six-pack of Cokes. She lifted the egg out of the canister, then placed it inside the cooler.

What was she doing? That egg belonged to Willie and his wife. It needed to stay in the nest. We were going to have a baby whooping crane here in Texas for the first time in forever. And I'd get to name it. What would the cranes think when they got back to the nest and the egg wasn't there? I wanted to scream. I didn't care anymore that it would bother the cranes to hear my voice. Nothing could bother them more than seeing that their egg was missing. They wouldn't understand what had happened. They were good parents. Odetta said so.

I shook my head and whispered, "No, no, no, no, no," as Odetta closed the lid of the cooler and placed it in her bag. A thousand questions were stuck in my throat. I held them in, because if I opened my mouth they'd all come rushing out in one big scream, louder than the whooping cranes' calls.

I backed away from the wall, unable to watch anymore, and tried to block out the calls of the cranes. I wanted to punch something, even if one punch would send those rickety walls crashing to the ground. That would be okay with me. I wished I'd never gone to the old infirmary, never seen those cranes, never seen that mockingbird at Buc-ee's. He hadn't been calling my name anyway. He was just a bird making noise.

I was mad at everyone. Mad at myself for even coming here to camp. At Sage for telling me about zugunruhe. At the girls who'd wanted to go on that stupid excursion to the infirmary. Mad at the cranes for making me care so much.

I started toward the doorway, but Audrey put an arm out to stop me.

"Just let me go," I said. "I can't do this."

Audrey wrapped me in a hug and said, "No, it'll be okay."

How could she say that? Nothing was okay.

Emma whispered, "What is that?"

"Nina, look!" said Ant.

Audrey unfolded from the hug and said, "You need to see this. Really."

I stepped back to the wall, still not wanting to look but wondering what the others were talking about. Odetta was pulling something else out of the cooler.

"Is that . . . ?" It was hard to tell from where we were, and it didn't make sense. It looked like Odetta was putting an egg in the nest. Then she stood and flagged down Felicity and Travis, who kept their brooms up while backing away from the cranes. The team returned to the infirmary together and stood at the wall to look out at the marsh. The rest of us watched, too.

Willie approached the nest, followed by the girl crane. They looked down at the egg and nudged it with their beaks; then Willie sat down on it.

The three staff members smiled at each other, then changed out of their hip waders. Odetta waved for us to follow her. She'd probably tell us what was happening when we got back to the office, but I couldn't wait that long. Once we were on the main trail, I asked, "Odetta? What's going on?"

We all stopped walking, and Odetta said, "Their egg isn't viable. We suspected it might not be since it hadn't hatched yet, but I didn't know for sure until I checked."

"That's what you were doing with the thermos?" I asked.

"Right," said Odetta. "The way it floated in the water let me know we didn't have a live chick in there."

Emma asked, "So it's just . . . empty? Or what?"

"Not empty," said Odetta. "But not alive anymore."

"Why?" asked Georgie.

"Yeah, what happened?" asked Ant.

"We don't know yet," said Odetta. "We'll take it back and examine it, and see what answers we get."

I shook my head. "But . . . they were good parents. You said so." I tried not to sound like a little kid, or like I was blaming Odetta. I didn't know what else to say.

"They were," said Odetta. "They are. That's why we brought a replacement egg to give them."

"Where did that egg come from?" asked Georgie. "Doesn't it belong to some other cranes?"

Travis said, "It's from an abandoned nest. We don't know why the parents didn't stay with it, but they had two viable eggs."

"And you know every egg is valuable," added Felicity. "When that happens, we collect the eggs to raise in captivity or to give to cranes whose eggs didn't make it."

We continued walking as we talked more. "They won't notice that the egg isn't theirs?" I asked.

"If they notice, they don't care," said Odetta. "Sometimes we even have an egg that hatches before we get to the nest, but we just put the new chick out there and the parents raise it like it's their own. Usually, I mean. That's why we waited to see if they'd go back to the nest."

"When is this egg supposed to hatch?" asked Ant. I hadn't thought of that. If we had to wait another month, summer camp would be over by then.

Odetta smiled and said, "Any day now."

Audrey invited the team to cool off in our cabin before they left. We all sat around the living room, drinking lemonade and talking about camp and the cranes.

"Any ideas why this egg didn't survive?" asked Georgie.

"Many eggs don't make it," said Odetta. "And many new cranes don't make it, either. That's even harder, when we see them hatch, see them walking around with their parents, and then lose them. Lots of reasons it happens—predators, disease, floods. As for the eggs, the odds get better as the parents get older. Experienced parents have more successful nests." She pointed toward the marsh. "This was their first try. First try together, anyway. Even though we don't know the mom's history, Willie's never nested with anyone before. There's plenty to celebrate, even though their own egg didn't survive. And now they'll get some experience as parents, which gives them an even better chance next year."

I was happy about the new egg, and that Willie and his wife were still on the nest. But I was sad at the same time. I'd been watching that first egg for the past month, already thinking about it as part of Willie's family. Already thinking about the new crane, who would be named Nina. Now it sat in a cooler in the back of a van.

"How do you do it?" I asked. "You care about them so much. . . ." I was upset enough over this one egg not making it; I couldn't imagine going through that again. If something bad happened to our marsh couple, I didn't think I could look at another whooping crane again.

"It hits us hard when bad things happen," she said. "But because we care about them, we keep going. Even in one of the rough seasons, like last year—we had twenty eggs hatch, and only five of those chicks survived. But that's five more whooping cranes in the world. We can't dwell on the ones we lost, the ones that get sick, that disappear after a storm or get shot down by a poacher."

"And sometimes we lose track of them for good," said Travis, "and we never know what happened."

"Those are the hardest for me," said Felicity, "when

they just disappear, and we don't know why. After so much time goes by, we have to assume they're not coming back."

"That would be rough," said Audrey. "The not knowing."

"What's even worse," said Odetta, "is when our own mistakes cause a problem. Even experts with the best intentions have made missteps. New cranes imprint on people who take care of them, as if those are their parents. They grow up not recognizing that they're cranes. Now we wear baggy white outfits when we're working with the hatchlings so we look more like shapeless blobs than humans."

"And having sandhill cranes sit on whooping crane eggs seemed like a good idea at the time," added Felicity. "There are a lot more sandhills than whoopers, and they're close in size. One project used them as surrogate parents for a while. But the hatchlings imprinted on the sandhills, and stayed with that flock. They wouldn't pair up with other whooping cranes in the wild."

"We've learned some things that don't work," said Odetta, "but we didn't know until someone tried. We've had to figure things out as we go along. Then we learn from our mistakes and adjust."

"If we were too afraid of making a mistake," said Travis, "we wouldn't do anything. And we'd have no whooping cranes at all. It hurts to lose any of them, but if we put too much hope in one bird or one egg, we lose sight of the whole flock."

"I still wish we'd found out who the mother crane is," I said. "We really tried."

"We still want to solve that mystery!" said Odetta. "She and Willie Nelson might stay together for the rest of their lives. It'll be great to find out who she is, and whatever else we can learn about her. And you girls did help us. Remember, you're the reason we know about the cranes at all. Without you, we wouldn't have known to bring a new egg for these parents."

"All thanks to you girls breaking the rules," said Audrey.

"We had to visit the haunted infirmary!" said Emma.

"Right," said Ant. "It was more like following a tradition than breaking a rule."

"Oh yeah," said Odetta. "I was so excited about the cranes, I forgot we were out there in a haunted cabin!"

That got us all laughing, and we filled in the crane staff on Josephine's story.

"I guess it's really thanks to Josephine that we discovered the cranes," I said.

Odetta held up her lemonade glass and said, "To Josephine."

We all raised our glasses and toasted the girl who'd

led to our discovery, the one who had watched over the whooping cranes in this marsh.

"To Josephine."

Before the crane staff drove away, I asked if I could take a picture of the egg. I wanted a way to keep it with me, after putting so much hope into it. Odetta opened the back of the van and lifted the cooler out of the duffel bag. She'd put the egg inside a foam can koozie, just the right size to cradle it. Odetta pulled the egg out of the koozie and set it down. As many times as I'd seen it in trail-cam photos or through a hole in the infirmary wall, I'd never seen the egg up close. It was about four inches long, with dark brown spots scattered around the tan shell.

"Every whooping crane is significant," I said. "I read that somewhere."

"It's true," said Odetta. "We wish they could all survive, but that's not how nature works."

I took some pictures of the egg with my phone. "Audrey says that sometimes when things blow up, you still can find something worth saving."

"I like that. We'll learn what we can from this one, and we'll know a little more about these cranes."

We thanked each other and promised to keep in

touch. We'd be talking again really soon, since I had a new baby crane to watch for.

I waved at the team as they drove away with that egg named Nina.

Before going to bed that night, I added the egg to my notebook. I drew it as I'd first seen it, in the middle of the nest. The outline looked a little wobbly, but maybe I could fix it with some crayons or colored pencils later. I added a scattering of dark spots to the eggshell, then wrote below the picture *Because you were here, a whooping crane will hatch in Bee Holler, Texas.* That was true about the egg, and Josephine, and about me, too.

Chapter 29

From then on, I found it harder to wait for our infirmary trips. I wanted to be out there all the time, watching for movement in the nest. We didn't take turns anymore since no one wanted to miss anything. The four of us Oddballs hiked to the marsh with Audrey each time. One or both of the crane parents were always at the nest, seemingly unaware that the egg wasn't their own. Or, like Odetta said, they didn't care. They were good parents, and had a baby crane on the way.

Even though Odetta had said that the egg would hatch any day now, I couldn't help worrying about it. All those things that could go wrong kept popping into my head.

Three days after Odetta's visit, we watched both parents calling out together, Willie with his long *whooooops* and the female crane's short *whoop whoop*s. With both of them at the nest, we couldn't get a view of the egg. We'd have to rely on the trail cam to show us how it was doing.

"Odetta will love this," I said, "the two of them putting on a show."

"It's a great concert," said Ant. "I'll grab the memory card."

"Wait," said Audrey. "Look at that." She handed me her binoculars. Willie had stepped aside, giving us a better view of the nest.

"Is something there?" asked Georgie.

"I think so!" said Emma.

Something was in the middle of the nest. Not the egg, but something cinnamon-brown and fuzzy. Feathers. Cinnamon feathers on a little crane head.

I almost cried with relief. At the same time, I laughed. I didn't need anything to translate the crane calls. They were celebrating. The group of us watching from the infirmary celebrated, too—quietly, for the moment. We high-fived each other, then shared a group hug. Ant gave a quiet "Whoop, whoop!" and we all laughed.

Before leaving, we looked out at the marsh once more. I told Aunt Audrey and my friends, "Say hi to the first whooping crane to hatch in Texas in over a century!"

*   *   *

After dinner that night, I asked Audrey if we could go to the art barn.

"Really?" she said. "Yeah, that'd be great. What do you want to work on?"

"Just some coloring. I'll get my notebook."

Once we got to the art barn, Audrey took out the watercolor painting supplies for herself, and the crayons and colored pencils for me. We sat across from each other again at one of the tables while we worked. After coloring the tan shell and brown spots of the crane egg, I turned to a new page. I'd watched the cranes so much during the past month, maybe I could draw one. It might not be very good, but I'd give it a try. Nothing would blow up.

I scrolled through a few pictures on my phone and zoomed in on a good photo of the mother crane's face. I'd start there, maybe just the eye, the curve of black feathers in front of it, and the patch of red on the head.

"So, how excited was Odetta about the hatchling?" Audrey asked. I'd called Odetta right after we got back from the infirmary, and sent her the latest photos and videos from the trail cam.

"Really excited. She called out to the staff, 'Come see our Texas baby!' and there was a lot of cheering in the background."

"I'll bet," said Audrey. "It's a big deal."

"She said they're looking forward to coming back in

a few months, to put on tags and trackers and get blood samples. Maybe I could come back then, too?"

"Of course. Makes sense you should be here. I'm sure Odetta would love to see you again."

"I just hope the new crane will be okay. Odetta said once it's three months old, it'll have a really good chance of survival." As happy as I was about the crane chick, I was also holding my breath, waiting to see if it would survive and grow as big as its parents. "Until then, it's hard not to worry."

"I get that," said Audrey. "Nature can be rough. Lots of challenges for something that small. But like Odetta said, they're good parents, right? Willie and his wife will do all they can to take care of their new baby."

I stopped coloring and looked out the window, like there was an answer out there to a question that hadn't formed yet. Something was bothering me—not just the worry about the baby crane. It felt like I was forgetting something. What was it? Something to do with what Odetta and the others said about why some cranes don't survive. I turned to a new page to scribble what I remembered. *Predators, hunting, storms, illness.* Felicity had said that sometimes the cranes disappear. After enough time passes, the staff have to accept that a missing crane isn't coming back and they won't ever know what happened to them. I also remembered what Emma said about solving a mystery. It happens when the detective discovers what they've overlooked all along.

Maybe Audrey was right about working on an art project while trying to figure something out.

"Everything okay?" said Audrey.

I stood up and tossed the crayons into the bin. "I need to check on something."

"What?"

"Something my brain just put together."

Back in the cabin, I ran to my room with Audrey's laptop. I sat with my fingers on the keyboard and took a deep breath. I tried not to get my hopes up. This might not change anything. *It's probably nothing. But it could be something.*

I'd been in such a hurry to narrow down who the girl crane was, maybe I narrowed it down too much. This time, I started at the end of the yearbook. The crane staff couldn't look away when sad things happened, and I wouldn't either. I checked the graphs of every crane's call, without skipping any.

At the top of the last page, I found it. The peaks and valleys of the voiceprint we'd been looking for. I printed out the graph to make sure.

After grabbing the printout from the living room, I placed it over the mother crane's graph and held them up to the light. The lines matched up.

Odetta had mentioned this crane once, that first

time we called her. I looked at the yearbook entry again, and clicked on a link beneath her photo. The article that came up looked familiar. I'd skipped it before, not wanting to see what had happened to those cranes, and what had caused such pain in Odetta's face. But now I did read it.

The article was from a year earlier, about four whooping cranes who were shot down. Whoever did it was never caught and didn't even take the birds, but left their bodies where they fell. The people who worked so hard to protect the cranes were devastated. With such a small population, the loss of four cranes was a huge blow. The Wildlife and Fisheries staff collected the carcasses of Martha, Maurice, and Dodger. The body of a fourth crane was never found. Some of the blood and feathers at the scene matched her DNA, and no one ever saw her again or picked up a reading from her tracker. They guessed a predator had dragged her away.

But she wasn't dragged away. She'd been injured, then somehow made it out of there on her own. No telling where she'd been wandering around since then, but I knew where she was now.

I'd wanted so much to find out this crane's name, and there it was in front of me.

Holy buckets, we found Dolly Parton.

Emma answered the door at the Oddballs cabin. "I think I found her," I said.

We sat on the floor together with the printouts of the graphs. "I checked the yearbook again after I got the idea that we'd overlooked something. Could this be right?"

They passed around the printout of the yearbook page and compared it with the graph of the crane mom's voice.

"Whoa," said Ant. "They do match."

"But . . . how?" said Emma.

"When I searched the yearbook this time, I didn't ignore the cranes who were presumed dead."

"Because presumed dead isn't the same as for-sure dead?" said Georgie.

"Right. If a whooping crane hasn't been seen for a long time, people who work with them assume they're dead. Most of the time they're right—huge birds like that can't hide easily, plus they have the trackers."

"But sometimes . . . ?" said Ant.

"Sometimes, maybe a crane hangs around where no one is looking."

"Like here?" asked Emma.

"Exactly like here," I said.

"Odetta mentioned this crane that time we called her, right?" said Georgie.

"Yeah, she said they used to have a Dolly Parton," said Emma.

I showed them the poaching article. "It makes sense that everyone thought she didn't make it."

"What about her tag and tracker?" asked Emma. "How did those disappear?"

"The article said none of the cranes had them when they were found. Whoever shot the cranes probably cut off the tags and trackers and destroyed them, to get farther away from the scene before anyone found the cranes."

Ant read some of the article out loud, then said, "Dolly must've been hurt, but she got away somehow."

"And at some point, she met Willie," I said, "and they ended up here."

"This is amazing!" said Georgie. "I can't believe she survived that."

"So she and Willie are from the same flock after all," said Emma. "You're as good a detective as Nessie McGee, Nina! Sorry if my idea about the lost crane was a red herring."

"No, it's okay," I said. "It was a good guess. Like you said, we had to look at all the clues."

"Can you imagine what Odetta will say when she finds out Dolly is here?"

Odetta would be even happier than we were about this news. She'd known Dolly her whole life, and thought she'd lost her forever. "I can't wait to tell her," I said. "I'll call in the morning and let her know that our mystery crane is no longer a mystery."

Chapter 30

Odetta couldn't believe it when I told her we'd found a match. I didn't tell her who the crane was—I wanted her to see for herself. Convincing her that Dolly Parton was alive and well and a new mom might not be easy.

"How did we miss it before?" she said.

"I'll show you. There's even bigger news, too."

"Bigger than finding out who the mystery crane is? Okay, let's see it."

"Bring up the crane yearbook and go to the last page. You'll see a graph that matches the one I just sent you of the mother crane's call."

After some key clicking, Odetta said, "Okay, scrolling through the graphs, and . . . Hold it. This can't be. Dolly?"

"She survived, Miss Odetta. I know she was hurt— I read about what y'all found there, afterward." I stopped myself before going on. I'd been so excited about the voiceprint match, I hadn't stopped to think about how Odetta would feel. This happy news was also a reminder of that awful day, when she saw those cranes that someone shot down from the sky. How much worse would that feel than finding out the egg wasn't going to hatch? The staff had known and cared about and watched over those four cranes from the time they were new eggs in a nest. When they found out they'd been killed and had to collect what was left on the ground, they must have been heartbroken and angry at the same time.

This wasn't about showing I could do something right, or finding out the crane's name. Right then, I just wanted to give Odetta this news about a crane she loved. "I'm so sorry about what happened. That someone did that to them, and that you lost those cranes. But Dolly Parton got away. She's here."

That night after dinner, I called Iris to update her. I wanted to talk about something else, too, that had nothing to do with cranes. Well, it did have to do with the cranes, in a way. Because we'd worked on the crane calls together, I finally felt confident enough to bring up what had been on my mind.

I caught her up as best I could, then signed to her, *Thanks again for your help.*

She shrugged, then wrote, *Sure, working with those voiceprints was interesting. You probably could've done all that yourself, though.*

"Maybe," I said. "But I don't know, you're really good at that stuff, like noticing sound patterns. No one else noticed the different ways the cranes call out."

Iris smiled and added, *Yeah, you needed the Deaf girl to tell you what the cranes sounded like.*

I could sign the next thing I wanted to say, if I took my time. *Also, I knew you'd understand.* From the start, Iris had seemed to know why I wanted to help the cranes.

That's true, she signed. *I understood.*

I'd wanted to reconnect with Iris, too. The cranes just gave me a good reason to do it. We were sort of friends now. This was my chance to fix what I'd done wrong before.

"Hey," I said, trying to look like this idea just occurred to me, "have you ever thought about transferring back to Timber Oaks? It'd be so great to get to see you again at school every day."

A glance at Iris's face told me the answer. I tried to look like whatever she said next would be okay, no matter how much it would hurt.

Oh, that's really nice, she wrote, *but I love Bridgewood.*

I'm sorry, I signed, then lowered my hands because

it looked like Iris had more to say. We each motioned for the other to go ahead, then laughed a little.

"I should've respected your space," I said. "I wanted to talk to you, and I made a mess of things. If you come back, I promise things will be different." My voice cracked, and the auto-captions missed some of what I'd said. I typed in the chat to fill in the gaps, then sat on my hands to keep from adding more. Iris had to see that I was serious. She'd seen how I communicated better, that I took time to step back and watch and listen and was respecting boundaries.

No, it really isn't about you, Iris typed. *Yeah, you didn't make it any easier.* The smile she gave me helped to ease the sting of her words. *But I didn't switch schools because of any one thing or one person. It was everything. And now I have this place where I really belong. I'm happy there.*

I smiled back at Iris and signed to her, *I'm really happy for you.* And that was true, but I wished she could've been happy at my school. Then I felt selfish. Why couldn't I just be happy for Iris without being sad at the same time?

But this has been good, Iris continued. *I liked working on the crane calls with you. I'm glad you got in touch.*

Me too, I signed.

Looks like you've found a place where you belong, too, right? Like you've found your flock.

"Is that a bird joke?" I asked.

Yeah, I'm a real hoot.

I rolled my eyes but smiled, too. "You and Ant would really get along." I thanked Iris again, then asked, "Okay if we stay in touch after I get back?"

Of course, she answered. *Next time you're in the tree across the street, hop down and say hi.*

Oh no. My face burned. "Wait, you know about that?"

Iris laughed, but it didn't look like she was laughing at me. It felt more like we were sharing a joke. I laughed, too.

And thanks for telling me about that whale and nightingale song, she continued. *It's amazing. Two completely different animals, but they sort of have the same language.*

"Yeah," I said, "it's nice how that works out sometimes."

I stayed overnight with the Oddballs one more time. Camp was coming to an end, and we weren't ready to say goodbye. After lunch on the last day, goodbyes were happening all over the place, with plenty of crying, laughing, hugging, and promises to keep in touch. When I came across Cecilia, she was laughing, but her face was red and damp like she'd been crying, too. She'd been coming to camp every year since she was ten years old, and this day would be her last one. Last one as a camper, anyway. She'd probably come back as a counselor. Maybe I would, too. We'd watch the campers sneak out to the haunted infirmary, thinking they were keeping a big secret from us.

Cecilia smiled when she saw me and said, "Wikipedia!" and gave me a hug. "I'm so glad you got to come here this summer."

"Really? I mean, yeah, me too. It's been fun. And thanks for leading us out to the infirmary. That was really interesting."

She laughed again and said, "Scary, too, thinking we saw a ghost!"

Odetta said that Willie and Dolly would probably continue nesting in the same area every year. The marsh would have its ghosts for a long time.

Later, in the Oddballs cabin, I helped the girls pack up the last of their things. Emma gave me one of her books, *Nessie McGee and the Missing Penguin.*

"Thanks, Emma," I said. "You're sure you want to give this away?"

"Yeah, I've read it so much I have it memorized," she said. "I think you'll like it, since you're pretty good at solving mysteries, too."

We'd all exchanged phone numbers so I could update them on any crane news. Also so we could just talk sometimes, since we were friends. "I'll ask Audrey if we can plan an Oddballs reunion, like whenever Odetta comes back to check on the cranes and tag them."

"That'd be perfect!" said Emma.

"If you can't make it, I'll send you pictures," I said. "But it'll be better if all the Oddballs are together."

"And let us know how you and Iris are doing," said Georgie, "after you get home."

"I will. She said it seems like I found my flock here, with all of you."

"That Iris is pretty smart," said Ant.

I looked around the cabin, not finding anything else to pack. The girls' bags were ready to go. "Need help carrying anything to the pickup area?"

"No," said Ant. "But come with us anyway."

Zugunruhe works in both directions. One way I was different from Audrey was that I wouldn't want to live at camp year-round. I'd had so much fun, but I was ready to migrate back home. It'd been a long time since I'd listened to the birds in my backyard. Maybe they missed me, too, like Sage said.

As I was packing my bag, I came across the wildlife list Audrey had given me when I first got to camp. I'd planned on checking off so many bird sightings, but most of the spaces were blank. That didn't bother me.

I'd gotten to see birds that weren't even on the list. At the bottom of the page, I wrote *Whooping crane* and made a big checkmark.

I couldn't believe how big the twins looked when my family arrived. In just the few weeks I'd been away, they'd stopped looking like babies. "Look at those big kids!"

"Nina!" said Chloe, then Aiden echoed her. "Nina!" They ran right into me for a big hug.

"I've missed you so much!" I said. I even got hugs from Sage and Declan.

"We've missed you, kid," said Dad.

Mom brushed my hair back and said, "Look at you. It's like you've grown up while you were here."

"It hasn't been that long, Mom!" I laughed, but maybe I looked to her like the twins looked to me, so much older after just a summer.

"I'm so proud of you," she added. "I couldn't have stayed here all summer. I wish I could be more like you, taking on something so . . . outdoorsy."

I didn't know what to say to that. I'd never imagined my mom wishing she could be like me in any way. Maybe we just liked different things, and that was okay.

"Well," I said, "you'll be happy to know I took some time for flower arranging. This way to dinner."

In the dining lodge, I introduced everyone to Estelle

and the rest of the staff. Earlier, I'd borrowed ceramic vases from the art barn and picked wildflowers to put in them for centerpieces.

Back when camp started, I missed my seat at the staff table, and wanted the place to ourselves again. Now the dining lodge was weirdly quiet and empty without all the campers. I missed the songs and laughter and chatting that had filled the big room.

I showed my family the containers of the pizza toppings and gave the instructions. "Grab a pizza crust and put whatever you want on it. Then we'll bake them in the kitchen."

"That's a lot of toppings," said Declan.

"Try the fig and onion," I said, "and thank me later."

We could've stayed there all night, catching up on our summers and trading slices of pizza. The best part was seeing Aunt Audrey and Mom talking and laughing together. They were so different, it was hard to believe they'd come from the same family. But there was something worth saving.

"I need to show you something before we leave," I said. "It's where I spent a lot of time this summer. You'll see why."

On our walk to the old infirmary, I told them about the cranes, and why it was such a surprise they were here. "We'll use quiet voices," I told Chloe and Aiden, "so we won't scare them."

Everyone got to see the whole crane family, since both Willie and Dolly were at the nest with their new hatchling. I held Chloe in my arms and Sage held Aiden while we showed them where to look.

"Big birds!" said Chloe.

"Right, they're so big! There's Willie. He's the daddy. The mommy bird is Dolly. And who do you think that little one is?"

"Baby!" said Aiden.

"That's right, the baby bird."

Declan asked, "What's the baby's name?"

"That's Josephine. I got to name her."

"Josephine?" said Sage.

"Yeah. Well, JoJo for now, at least until we find out if it's a boy or a girl."

"How'd you pick that?" asked Mom.

JoJo called out a squeak, and the parents joined in for a family chorus.

Dad laughed and said, "They must know we're talking about them."

"Josephine is the reason I found the cranes." When it had come time to tell Odetta what I wanted to name the new crane, I'd thought back to what Libby had said before our first nature walk, and how she called them Florence hikes as a way to tell others about a woman more people should know about. I'd been thinking about the girl who'd watched over the cranes when she lived here so long ago. I thought more people should know about her.

Later, I'd tell my family more about Josephine and the whooping cranes. Probably more than they ever wanted to know. But for now, my family would watch and listen to the crane family, together in this good birdy place.

Acknowledgments

Many whoops of thanks to the flock:

Editor Kelsey Horton at Delacorte Press for her guidance, support, and endless patience while I worked on this story. And to the whole Random House Children's Books team: managing editor Tamar Schwartz, vice president and publisher Beverly Horowitz, copyeditor Colleen Fellingham, trade marketer Catherine O'Mara, marketing designer Michael Caiati, Erica Stone and Adrienne Waintraub of school and library marketing, publicist Kathy Dunn, and everyone who's worked to make this book stronger and to share it with readers.

My outstanding agent, Molly O'Neill, for being the perfect champion for my work and for the brainstorming sessions that give birth to story ideas. I couldn't ask for a better partner to have by my side.

Foreign rights agent Heather Baror-Shapiro of Baror International for working to bring my books to audiences around the world.

Illustrator Leo Nickolls, art director Liz Dresner, and designer Suzanne Lee for the gorgeous book cover.

Jenna Beacom, for reading the manuscript to check for linguistic and Deaf culture accuracy. Sara Zimorski and Eva Szyszkoski of the Louisiana Department of Wildlife and Fisheries, Anne Lacy of the International Crane Foundation, Dr. Bernhard Wessling, and author Gary Clark, nature columnist for the *Houston Chronicle*, for answering whooping crane questions I had along the way. Special thanks to Sara and Bernhard for reading the manuscript to check for accuracy and offer additional feedback.

Any factual errors in the novel are my own.

My writing community: the Will Write For Cake critique group, the "Lodge of Death" retreaters, and the SCBWI. This writing road can be a lonely and bumpy one, and I can't imagine traveling it without you.

My family and friends for the encouragement and support.

Thank you all for helping this book take flight.

Finally, I'd like to thank the other middle-grade authors who have joined me in reserving space in their books to honor the victims of the tragic school shooting at Robb Elementary in Uvalde, Texas, that took twenty-one lives. Most of the victims were the very children we write stories for, and their own stories ended way too soon. All admiration goes to the families of the victims who fight tirelessly to hold our state and federal officials accountable to make schools safer for all children and educators. You can find ways to support them at livesrobbed.com.

LYNNE KELLY is the award-winning author of *Song for a Whale,* which won the Schneider Family Book Award and was named a Best Book of the Year by the New York Public Library. She lives near Houston, Texas, with her dogs, Abigail and Eloise.

lynnekellybooks.com